Waltz of the Hunter

By

Matthew Kitsell

Story consultant:
Matthew J Gunn

For Matt and Jimmy,

Who love all the same stories that I do...

PROLOGUE

The beautiful bronze girl lay motionless, face down in the white sand. Not a muscle on her magnificent body twitched. The gentle winds blowing in from the Pacific gently ruffled her luxurious, dark amber hair. Her slender arms were spread proudly out in front of her, her fingers delicately caressing the white sand. Her firm, muscular legs stretched out towards the water, the waves calmly lapping at her toes. The red, Hawaiian sun delicately kissed her back as it lowered itself slowly below the Pacific horizon.

Nothing moved. There was no sound at all apart from the soothing roll of the waves quietly lapping onto the beach. There was something unnaturally, eerily still about the scene. If there had been another human being looking down upon the girl, they might have assumed that she was dead.

A Hawaiian honeycreeper perched nonchalantly in a nearby cluster of palm trees suddenly stood erect on its hind legs. Its head whipped around, startled.   No sound broke the peace of the scene, but the honeycreeper knew that something, or someone, was close.   It raised itself further, preparing to break cover from the trees.   The girl's body remained still.   A full minute passed before the honeycreeper could bear it no longer and suddenly exploded into the sky, taking several of its flock with it.

A scratching sound came from a sandy path leading down to the beach.   A dark, ominous shadow suddenly spread across the sand, followed by the figure of a tall, brown, young man.   He stood under the shade of a Jacaranda tree, his eyes gazing incuriously down the beach onto the girl.   Clad in a white T-shirt and a pair of black shorts, the young man was, like the girl, a native of Maui, and a figure of rare and exceptional beauty.   Despite being a mere twenty-one years old, however, there was a discernible hardness in his posture and around his eyes.   A cigarette dangled lazily between the fingers of his left hand. The majesty of the scene meant nothing to him.   A sudden flash of disdain appeared in his eyes, and he leaned forward.   He called out.

"Leilani!"

The beautiful girl did not stir.   The boy shook his head and called out again, louder, and higher this time.

"Leilani!"

There was still no flicker from the girl.   The boy flicked his cigarette into the air, watching it cartwheel before dropping on to the sand.   He then started jogging on to the beach, his right foot stamping out the cigarette as he did so, his feet leaving a careless trail of footprints.   He stopped at the girl's side, staring down at her spectacular body.

"Leilani?" His voice was quiet, almost loving, but it did nothing to prompt any movement from the girl.   The corners of his mouth turned upwards nastily.

An eyebrow then flickered for an instant.   A moment later the girl's body stirred into life. She lifted herself with an exaggerated slowness to her knees and stared up at the boy, her deep brown eyes boring into his with a wild, savage hatred. She let her arms drop to her side, exposing the natural beauty of her body. Then she grabbed at a white shirt that she had been using as cushion and slowly put it on.

"He wants you," he told her. Angrily, she grabbed a towel that was lying to the side of her and got to her feet. She strode haughtily ahead of the boy, anxious to escape his horrible shadow. The path led up from the beach, winding uphill. To the right, the grassy bank sloped steeply away down to the waves crashing against the shore. The sweet, honey smell of the Pacific evening was being carried upwards by the warm, gentle winds. A flock of birds squawked with delight and then circled away into the sunset. Despite her efforts, Leilani could not distance herself from her unwelcome companion.

Soon she turned the final corner and at the top of the hill came to view the flat building that she had come to loath and despise with such ferocity that words could never adequately describe it. As a piece of real-estate, it reeked of decadent luxury and hideous wealth and, to her mind, was the most horrifying and evil-looking building she had ever seen. For the building had in her mind become inseparable from the terrible man who had created, financed, and was now putting the finishing touches to it; the man who had become her lover, protector and, very quickly after that, her tormentor in the two years that she had known him. The three roles had now blurred into one. The boy walked past her, grabbing her arm as he did so. She cried out, cursing him, and pulled away from him. He just leered at her and pointed towards the house. Obediently she walked ahead of him. She knew what was coming now and it would be more terrible and painful than words could describe. She always knew when it was that time because it was on those occasions when he would send the boy to fetch her. Sometimes he would allow the boy to stay and watch, which only added to the horror and humiliation.

Keonaoma.

Sweet fragrance.

That was the boy's name and that was the meaning. How wrong could a name be for an innocent boy born into this world? Sweet fragrance? He always smelled of sweat, cigarette smoke and, on occasion, dried blood.   He loved to watch and as the ritual began, he would lean back against the doorway, his arms folded, his cigarette permanently dangling from his lips, and giggle like an innocent child enjoying a new toy that he had just unwrapped.

She walked around the side of the expansive house. The tiles of the roof were of a shocking pink colour as though some giant hand had crudely applied a coat of paint to them.   The bungalow stretched out like a lazy lizard. On the south side of the house stood three men.   She stood a distance away.   Keomaoma was a few feet behind her, lurking at the corner of the house like a watchful night owl. She could hear the men talking in low voices.   The man in the middle was making expansive gestures with his arms and gesturing towards the ground.   The two men, one either side of him, were nodding and then making their own gestures in return. They were dressed in white suits and wore straw Panama hats.   They looked like attorneys, the sort of men who would spend their evenings in the most exclusive gaming clubs. Then the man in the middle turned and looked back towards her.

John Patrick Lomax smiled the most tender of smiles. She gave back the smile that she had practised in front of the mirror so many times over so many evenings, the smile that carried nothing behind it but pure technique, the smile that she hoped would be enough to get her through another evening. In that moment, she had to admit to herself, he looked like the kindest and most eligible of suitors. This was the Lomax that she had first known and fallen for. The other Lomax was the one she knew she would never get away from. The one time that she had managed to escape from this place he had found her again a mere twenty-four hours later and the punishment then had been beyond imagination. The boy had watched and giggled into the early hours of the morning.

There were of course the lengthy periods when Lomax went back to England where she understood he was some sort of high-ranking policemen. She lived for these periods but even when he was gone the security staff remained. There were only two of them, but they were always armed. They had never spoken a word to her and would merely glance at her occasionally with a momentary condescension. She understood only the odd word of French and both men spoke little English. Lomax seemed to have recruited them from the French army. They both shared the swarthy features and shifty looks that seemed to go with men of their type. Though she could not always see them, she knew they were there.

And then there was the boy. He never seemed to go anywhere. He was Lomax's cook but served more of a function as his sexual plaything. In fact, Lomax often showed more affection to him than he did to her. She would escape from the boy at night by locking herself in her room. On the occasional day he would amuse himself by taunting her until he finally got bored and left her alone. He never tried to touch her. Lomax would never have allowed that. If he had tried the guards would surely have reported him and then Lomax would have doled out a severe punishment for him too, bringing him down to the same level as her. On most days however the boy could be found in the straw-roofed hut on the beach with his buddies, endlessly smoking marijuana, drinking cheap beer, playing cards, and laughing at their

obscene jokes. He was never a problem
when he was with them. He was always
far, far worse whenever Lomax was
around.

Despite lacking height (he was five
foot seven) Lomax's body was taut and
muscular with only his stomach starting to
soften around the midriff. He had just
crept past fifty years of age and had
recently grown a luxurious moustache.
Chestnut brown hair crawled untidily
across his head from a side parting and his
eyes were as opaque as the blackest of
night skies. Once the smile left his face it
always hardened into an impenetrable
mask that gave nothing away. It
resembled a chiselled chunk of granite
with black slits for the eyes. Lomax
turned back to face his two companions.
He made a gesture of looking at his watch,
appearing preoccupied. Leilani saw him
shake his head in apology and then shake
the hands of both men. It was clearly time
for them to leave. They nodded, smiling
like alligators, and the men began walking
away towards the house, their figures
blending into the amber rays of the dying
sun.

The house. His life's dream. The culmination of everything for which he had worked and just the very idea of it chilled her to the bone. For she knew that he would soon be going away for the last time and once he had returned to this terrible paradise, she would never be rid of him. She had overhead him talking to these same men a week ago behind closed doors in the house; some serious business needed to be urgently taken care of back in England. It would be the last such job and would require four people besides himself, then he would back for good. *She would never be rid of him...* The boy had nearly caught her listening outside the door, but she had bolted at the sound of his footsteps.

She stood alone for a moment, looking out to the horizon, the thought crushing her soul.

The sun suddenly dipped below the horizon and a chilly wind was blowing. Leilani shivered and felt the familiar icy glove of terror clamp itself around the nape of her neck. Keonaoma had appeared behind her in the doorway leading to the patio. She could sense him leering at her.

"Hey Angel," his sweet, child-like voice crowed at her. She turned to face him. He was watching her, a savage grin on his face, his eyes leering lasciviously. He raised his hand and gently beckoned her indoors. There was nothing that she could do. She must go through it all again. She had survived every time so far and so she must survive it all again.

She must survive it.

She *must...*

Drawing a veil around her heart, she walked like an automaton back to the house and past the boy. She shut down. She felt nothing. She became nothing.

She walked through the large reception area tastefully decorated with wicker furniture and framed photographs of tropical fish. She walked past, not noticing, not caring, and slowly climbed the stairs. She came to the large, air-conditioned bedroom that she lived in terror of and walked inside.

Lomax was waiting there for her with his shirt off. The whip was in his hand already. He stroked it tenderly.

"On the bed," he ordered her softly, his eyes like empty slugs.

Keomaoma came in quietly behind her and closed the door. He lit a cigarette, and slowly inhaled. Then he blew out the smoke, watching it drift lazily to the ceiling. Leilani obeyed the command and lay down on her stomach. Lomax ripped the delicate fabric away from her back, exposing the soft, bronze, delicate skin.

"Darling girl," he murmured softly. Then he raised the whip.

The boy let out a childish squeak of delight and tittered.

The girl cried out in anguish.

And then the whip came down.

PART I

1

Tom Noonan looked out of the window of the small café on the edge of Ebury Street, the long, straight road that cuts a proud path through the heart of Belgravia, London, and felt the eyes of the other man on the back of his head. He had picked him out quickly after he had left the safehouse. He had stopped to look in a shop window and had caught his reflection in the glass. It had been a different man every time on the past three occasions, and Noonan had spotted all of them. This time it was a youngish man in a pale overcoat with a briefcase, looking every inch the junior accountant on his way to the office. He had blended in seamlessly with everything and everyone around him. Noonan had picked out at least two other young men who looked exactly like him. As usual, however, his inexperience had given him away. He had made one of the obvious mistakes: he had stopped at the exact same moment as Noonan on three separate occasions. He had known that Lomax would send someone to follow him. He had made two dummy runs earlier in the week just to test the opposition. The first time it had been an elderly man in a hat who inevitably moved faster than his age and appearance would suggest. The second time it had been a long-haired, moustachioed youth in a leather jacket. Three very different types of hounds then; the only thing they had in common was their penchant for elementary mistakes. Lomax had obviously needed to press them into service quickly as Noonan had had no trouble in outmanoeuvring them. The first two hounds he taken for a brisk walk around the park then back to the safehouse. Today was different though. Today it was vital that Noonan lost this man and made it appear entirely natural.

Casually, Noonan rose from the table, dropped a few coins on the tray and made his way to the door. He sensed the young man in the pale overcoat also rising from his corner. Noonan opened the door and stepped out into the busy street, feeling the breeze of the chilly February afternoon on his forehead. He turned and walked briskly towards the river. He weaved past all the bodies piling up in front of him. A bus growled angrily past him to his left. In front of it there was one taxi, one heavy goods vehicle, the end of the road and a set of traffic lights. Beyond that the road was clear. Noonan estimated distances, keeping his eyes fixed on the end of the road. He quickened his pace so that he was walking alongside the bus. The lights went from amber to red. The bus, stuck behind the lorry and the taxi, chugged to a halt. Noonan relaxed his pace and counted twenty seconds. The amber shone out and then the green. The lorry moved off followed by the taxi, which turned right. The bus ground into action and Noonan then suddenly ran out into the street. With incredible speed and dexterity, he leapt onto the bus as it was starting to pull away, grabbed the rail, swung himself in and collapsed down into the nearest available seat. As he had predicted, with a clear road ahead, the bus gathered speed. Noonan glanced in the mirror at the front of the bus. He could just make out the young man sprinting as fast as he could after the bus, gradually diminishing in size, eventually giving up the chase and throwing his hands out in frustration. Noonan smiled to himself. He wouldn't care to be in the young man's shoes when he had to report back to Lomax...

Five streets away, the bus ground away again leaving Noonan standing alone. He looked across to the old Norman church which seemed to stand remotely from everything else around it on the corner. Had Spender already arrived? Noonan crossed the street, jogged up the stairs to the large wooden doors, twisted the large round door handle and opened the door. He stepped into darkness. It was a dull day outside and not much light was getting in through the stained-glass window. Noonan shivered involuntarily. He peered through the darkness, seeing no-one. And yet he felt Spender's presence lurking somewhere in the gloom. The first time they had met in this place, two weeks previously, Noonan had sensed that Spender had arrived much earlier to check the place over thoroughly. He walked steadily into the small church, carefully looking into every corner and shadow. He reached the front of the nave and stood looking up at the coloured patterns on the window. A loud click sounded behind him, and he wheeled around. The door had been locked and still he saw no-one. He took a seat at the front and waited, worrying internally. Was it Lomax? Had he somehow found out about his meetings with Spender? If so, would he leave this place alive? He suddenly sensed the presence of a man seated directly behind him. He had not heard him approaching, no footsteps. He had appeared there as if by magic.

"It's been many years since I've paid my dues," rasped the gravelly voice behind him. "I'd hardly know where to start now."

Noonan turned in his seat and found himself looking into the same pair of hard, grey eyes that had seemed to devour him on the previous meeting and were devouring him still. The man was in his mid-sixties, with receding red hair, rapidly turning to grey. His skin was stretched taut over his face, his forehead creased in enquiry. His body was incredibly thin and wiry. He was wearing a thick overcoat which did little to disguise his thinness.

23

His body may have been showing signs of age, but the eyes still burned with a hard intelligence that suggested that his mind would not have slowed down in any way.

Noonan's body, taut and rigid, now relaxed. "Spender."

Spender took in the young man in front of him. His thick, chestnut brown hair was beginning to grow messily around his ears, and getting it cut was clearly not on his list of priorities. His eyes had the bloodshot look of someone who had not been sleeping well and had too much on his mind. The man was close to forty, his skin hardened from eking out a tough existence. He would start to age beyond his years quickly. Only the grey eyes felt incongruous, bathed as they were with warmth and empathy.

"What have you got for me?" Noonan could no longer suppress the urge to get to the heart of the matter. Spender however was clearly in no mood to be hurried. He smiled a thin, humourless smile.

"What have you got for me?" he simply repeated back to him. The facial muscles then relaxed into an expression of pure stone. Noonan would have to give.

"Lomax is putting a job together, a big one. Somewhere in the heart of London."

Spender seemed to lean forward slightly, his eyes narrowing earnestly. "Tell me."

Noonan shrugged apologetically. "Apart from working in a team with three others, that's all I've got."

"I see." Spender nodded once, his eyes burning into Noonan's, searching his mind to make sure that he was holding nothing back. Finally, he seemed satisfied. "Nothing at all about the other three?"

"Not yet." Noonan suddenly felt that the flow of information, flimsy as it was, was only going one way. It was time to get something in return. He leaned slightly into Spender. ""What about Anna?"

"Nothing yet, I'm afraid," Spender replied without sympathy. "But I'm using all the resources of my department to find her. You can be sure of that."

"Well, hurry up, will you?" Noonan pressed him urgently. "You know that Lomax is holding her somewhere. You find her, Spender, and I'll deliver Lomax."

"I'm going to give you a telephone number," Spender continued, as though he had simply not heard what Noonan had just said to him. "Memorise it: 01 709 4751. Repeat it, please."

"Don't worry, I'll remember it," Noonan replied, considering for a moment the pattern of the numbers and the sequence. After a few seconds, he knew he would never forget it.

"Call me as soon as you've got anything," Spender instructed him, getting up. He looked down imperiously at Noonan. "Don't mess this up, Noonan. Right now, I'm your only hope." Spender turned then and moved back down the nave towards the door. He seemed to glide as he moved, and the shadows swallowed him up. Then he reached the door and opened it. For a moment, the light framed him in the doorway, and Noonan caught a glimpse of his ghostly silhouette. But then with a loud clang the door closed, and he was gone.

Then it was Noonan's turn to stand up. He was glad to be going.

2

Alan Richard Spanton was on the run from the only thing in his life that he had ever genuinely loved – the British Royal Marines. Two months ago, he had been a Sergeant with the Commando regiment and the future looked bright, hopeful. Now, two months later, he was living like an animal in an abandoned warehouse and being hunted by his own people.

And all because someone had pushed him too far...

Alan Spanton's violent temper had been the source of most of his problems over the course of his life. And two months ago, it had scuppered his chances yet again. The Master-at-Arms had been pushing him too hard for too long. Finally, his nerves, his patience and his psyche had snapped, and he had gone for his Master-at-Arms. Five minutes later, the Master at Arms was on the floor with a broken neck. He had barely managed to flee the scene before the Royal Naval Police had turned up to formally arrest him for murder. Now they would be wanting the next thirty years of his life, and they were out searching for him now. But Alan Spanton did not much care for the idea of military prison. He preferred woodlands.

He had been on the move now for two months, sleeping rough in the woods, and moving on only after he had been spotted outside his bivouac by too many people with dogs throwing him curious glances. And curious passers-by might just inform their local police. So, it was always better to keep moving. He had found the warehouse a week ago and so far, he had seen no-one.

Spanton's eyes snapped open at six o' clock in the morning, his internal alarm clock waking him up on the dot as it always did. Forcing all feelings of tiredness out of his system, he lifted himself up, rubbed his eyes and wriggled out of the sleeping bag positioned amidst the rubble and dust in one corner of the warehouse. He stood up and looked wearily around the cold, harsh shell of the building, still bathed in blackness. It was vast and expansive with nooks and crannies going off on all sides. There was no ceiling, just iron beams spread horizontally across the sky that would once have supported a row of skylights.

If Alan Spanton had cared about such details, he would have remembered that this was the day that he turned thirty-five. But such personal data was of no consequence to him. Besides there would have been no-one to celebrate his birthday with. He had not shaved for a week and a thick growth of dark blond stubble had filled out his chin. His hair was blond and curly and had become a tangled mess during the time he had been living rough. His wide eyes were a striking pale green colour that seemed to blaze in darkened rooms. He had no siblings and his mother and father had both been killed when the Luftwaffe had dropped a bomb on their street in Brixton, destroying every house down one side of it. That had happened on the day he had turned four. He had never forgotten the terrible, ear-shattering blast that had echoed around his head for seemingly days (years?) afterwards; the dreadful, unending white noise; his room as it shook and tumbled all around him; his terrified screams; and finally, once the smoke and rubble had at last cleared the following morning, the smashed, scattered confusion of bones, blood and rags that had once been the bodies of his parents. That had set the tone for the rest of the birthdays to follow. And so, the boy Alan had grown up with neither anything to celebrate nor look forward to. That had quickly become normal.

Spanton's body suddenly snapped to attention. What was it? He remained still. Had he heard something? He listened. There was only silence outside, and yet he knew that something or someone was nearby. Then, from a distance away, he heard a voice calling out and a distant shuffle of feet. Noiselessly, he moved to the far corner of the warehouse, hurriedly rolling his sleeping bag up and stuffing it into his rucksack. He reached inside and pulled out the .9mm, checking the safety was on. He shoved it into his belt, shrugged the rucksack onto his back and crept to the empty side door of the warehouse. A row of torches was spread out across the grey curtain of the forest. Distant, muffled voices could be heard cutting through the chilly morning air. Spanton could smell police from a distance, and he instantly turned and ran to the far end of the warehouse, throwing himself through an empty space and out into the woods.

The forest was still in shadow though light was starting to break through in the sky. Visibility was poor and Spanton could only see about ten feet in front of him before the trees and bushes became blurry and indistinct. His feet plunged into a foot of mud and Spanton could feel the dampness soak through to his socks. His ears were questing for any tell-tale signs of his pursuers' progress. The sound he heard instantly dampened his spirits – dogs! He could hear their enthusiastic yapping increasing in volume as his trail had been sniffed out and found. Spanton estimated that he had been running for three minutes and that the police would now be at the warehouse. They would find the stuff that he had left behind and they would know then that he was close, but not how close. The dogs would have already picked up his scent and now the pursuit would get going for real.

Spanton's superb physical condition meant that he could run at a breakneck pace without flagging for a while. He breathed in and out in precise rhythm, like a heart machine. But he knew that the dogs would eventually catch up with him. This thought made him pick up his pace. Despite the temperature hovering around freezing, his face was already feeling flush with warmth, and he could feel a trickle of sweat running down his forehead. The ground beneath him became a quagmire. He could hear his feet squelching through the mud as he ran. He nearly slipped and fell backwards a couple of times. He descended a sharp bank to a small stream and jumped it, just managing to scramble up the far bank without sliding back down into the water. He listened again. The barking of the dogs was getting louder.

He saw a pair of headlights moving up ahead of him and then a road. A car swept past and was gone into the dark morning. A familiar white shape emerged from the left with its blue light blazing. Instantly Spanton dived back into the shadows.   The white police Land Rover swept past, bathing him in its blue light. He waited for it to pass by. But instead, it pulled over to the side of the road and waited. Had he been seen? Only one way to find out.

Spanton moved quickly through the shadows by the side of the road, reaching the white Land Rover in about forty seconds.   He pulled the .9mm out of his belt and snatched at the car door with his left hand. It swung open. The sound of static from a police radio filled the air. The shocked face of a sandy haired young police constable, no more than twenty-three years of age, stared out in shock at the .9mm that had been shoved in his face and the fixed, purposeful expression of the blackened, bearded face beyond it. Spanton said nothing, just gestured once with the gun.   The young constable understood and put the radio back in position, his eyes wide and pale with sudden terror. Spanton took a step back and beckoned the young constable out with the gun. Slowly the boy stepped down and onto the pavement. He clamped his hands behind his head.

"Turn," Spanton ordered him softly, the gun moving in an arc. The boy's mouth fell open and he started to breathe heavily, suddenly fearing the worst. Spanton lifted the gun and brought it down hard on the boy's head. He went down without a sound. He would come round in five minutes with a sore head. Though he had had to display the gun to get the young man out of the vehicle, he would never have fired it. He would never use his weapon against a member of the British police. He would only ever use it against enemies of her Majesty's forces, and there were enough of those already.

Hurriedly, Spanton climbed into the Land Rover, slammed the door, and floored the accelerator. The vehicle tore off down the narrow, winding lane, the blue lights still flashing. The radio crackled and spluttered incessantly. Spanton grabbed the cable and yanked it out, lobbing the broken receiver into the back seat. All was suddenly silent in the vehicle.

Five minutes later he reached a crossroads. A white police Rover suddenly shot out from the right. Spanton swerved to avoid it and took off down the left lane.

The Rover braked hard at an angle across the road. Spanton floored the accelerator again, taking the speed of the vehicle up to fifty. It took the Rover a few seconds to start up again and take off after him, its siren suddenly splitting through the damp morning air.

Spanton took a corner too fast and lost control of the vehicle. At the same time, a large brown estate car appeared from nowhere directly in front of him. A crash was inevitable. The horn from the estate screeched furiously at him. Desperately Spanton yanked the wheel to the left, forcing the vehicle out of the path of the oncoming estate and off the road. A second later the vehicle crunched sickeningly into an enormous beech tree, sending an earth-shattering jolt through the car. The windscreen disintegrated in front of Spanton, and his head slammed into the steering wheel.

Suddenly Spanton was swimming in an ocean of blurriness. The crash played through his mind again in slow motion. From somewhere, a thousand miles away, he could hear a siren and voices calling out. He desperately tried to shake himself free of the ocean. Thirty seconds later, he lifted his throbbing head, but it was too late. Two uniformed officers were leaning into the vehicle and hauling him out. His hand went for the gun at his belt, but it was no longer there. That had already been confiscated.

"Now, you bastard...!" the taller of the two uniformed police officers spat out. They spun him round, forced his hands behind his back and then the cuffs were on.

Two days had passed. Spanton was staring angrily at a biro mark on the wall of the small interview room in the Maidenhead police station. Possession of a weapon and the attack on the police constable had automatically meant that Scotland Yard had been called in from London. Two of their inspectors had been trying and failing for the last forty-eight hours to get anything out of him. In the Marines he had survived the harshest interrogation techniques. He knew that they would never break him. They had left him alone two hours ago and since then he had seen and heard no-one. So, he put his mind to escaping. So far, he had managed to keep his identity from them, but it would only be a matter of time before his picture was circulated and someone picked up on it. Time was running out. Whoever walked through the door next was going to get it. He had to get out of here...

There was the click of the door being unlocked. Spanton instinctively felt his body tense. The door swung open and a man he had not yet encountered was standing there, looking down on him with a mixture of curiosity and condescension. He carried himself with a natural authority and his dark eyes seemed to stare right through Spanton. He was wearing an expensive overcoat and looked like a man who would clearly out-rank everybody else in the police station. His body was hard like a bullet. He closed the door behind him.

"Alan Spanton," he just said quietly. "You're about to spend the next thirty years of your life behind bars."

Spanton remained in his seat, his right arm gripping the back of his chair. Who was this man? How had he identified him? He tried to suppress a familiar, sick feeling in his stomach. The stranger walked calmly into the room and stood over him.

"But I'm the one person who can stop you going to prison, if you do exactly as I say."

"Who are you?" Spanton asked quietly.

The stranger smiled a cruel, alligator-like smile, which stretched across his moustachioed face. "My name is Patrick Lomax."

Spanton looked into his eyes. When he spoke again, his voice sounded different, more vulnerable. "What do you want from me?"

Lomax leaned forward and offered him a cigarette. Spanton looked at the packet as though a puff adder might leap out of it and bite him on the fingers.

"Go ahead," Lomax reassured him.

Spanton carefully leaned forward and took a cigarette. He put it to his lips. Lomax threw him a box of matches. Spanton lit the cigarette, inhaled, blew the smoke up to the ceiling and looked back at Lomax thoughtfully.

3

John Brewster had almost everything he needed in his life right now: fifty thousand pounds in a briefcase and, very soon, the girl he loved and wanted to spend the rest of his life with. The only thing remaining was to make a clean getaway from the country with both. He had arranged for two fake passports to be made up, one for himself and one for Jean. These were also in the briefcase. The fifty thousand pounds amounted to his life's work. It was the money that he had managed to spirit away from his ruthless boss, Tony Caldwell, the most feared criminal in all South London, for all the various jobs he had undertaken for him over the years. That was not all he was spiriting away, for Jean had been Caldwell's girl for the last three years.

The eight fifteen train from St Albans on which he now travelled ground to a halt at platform eight of Euston Station. Immediately the doors swung open, and the morning commuters started piling out, almost tripping over each other in their rush to get ahead. The platform was quickly swarming with them, all wearing the uniform of the white-collar city worker, clad in raincoats, carrying briefcases and hurriedly rolled up newspapers.

John Brewster stepped off the train and quickly found himself caught up in the throng. He viewed the army of commuters with disdain, but his mind was excited. In twenty-four hours, he would be in New York with Jean, and from there they would board a one-way plane to their destination, Miami. From a distance, even in this crowd, John Brewster was easily noticeable, standing taller than most at six foot three, with a fine head of luxurious, chestnut brown hair swept back in a bouffant style. He was a strikingly handsome man in his mid-thirties, with careful, watchful blue eyes and a mouth that often curled upwards in quiet amusement at whatever situation he found himself in and at the general absurdity of life. A pair of tidy sideburns reached the bottom of his ears. He was wearing an expensive raincoat and the briefcase was a smart Algernon Asprey. Under his raincoat he wore a Savile Row suit. He wanted to look good for Jean. This was a special day.

Forty-five minutes later, his taxi arrived outside Jean's Hampstead townhouse ten minutes ahead of schedule, which pleased Brewster. Everything was going his way. He stepped out of the taxi, ordered the driver to wait, and trotted up the steps to the front door of the majestic townhouse. He flipped the Yale key that Jean had made up for him out of his pocket, slid it into the lock and let himself in. He closed the door softly behind him. Everything was in its place in the luxurious hallway. She was not there with her suitcase as he had expected. Brewster smiled and shook his head. She must still be in the bedroom putting the finishing touches to her face.

"Jean?" he called up the stairs. No sound came back down. He put his briefcase down and, noticing that she had not picked up her post, did so. There were the usual brown envelopes but on top was a sealed wallet containing recently developed photographs. He ripped the seal open and lifted the photographs out. Brewster suddenly felt icy tingles running down his back. He saw his own image on the first monochrome photograph, seated next to Jean; he recognised the table outside the restaurant where they had lunched two weekends ago; they had secretly arranged to meet at the coastal village in West Sussex; they were clasping each other's hands lovingly. Feeling a sickness rising in his throat, he leafed hurriedly through the rest of the photos. It got worse: their arms around each other, kissing outside the hotel; enjoying each other on the bed, this photograph snapped through the window from across the street, presumably from another hotel. Brewster felt his palms sweating and he pressed down hard on the photographs, creasing them. So, someone had found out! But how? They had been so careful! And now Caldwell knew...

There was something else... Post not collected! Jean always collected her post before breakfast, and that was always before eight o'clock. Silently, he placed the post and photographs down on a side table. His right hand slid into his overcoat pocket and pulled out the Walther PP pistol that he had been carrying since the previous afternoon. He flipped the safety off and stood like a statue in the hallway. The house was as silent as a tomb. He knew then that something was terribly wrong. He stepped forward silently, praying that the floorboards would not creak. He reached the door on the left leading into the drawing room. It was half open. He peered through the gap between the hinges. He raised his gun. Her handbag lay open on the edge of the sofa, half of its contents spilled out on the carpet. That same gut instinct that had kept him alive for years suddenly kicked in again, and he dropped to the ground. As he did so, a bullet slammed into the door frame where his head had been a fraction of a second earlier. Brewster swivelled on the balls of his toes and lifted his gun. The dark shape that had suddenly appeared at the top of the stairs was taking a second aim. Brewster fired twice. The body jerked, the arm rising upwards as if in an exaggerated gesture of a salute. The gun in the hand fired once into the ceiling and then the body toppled clumsily, messily, down the stairs. The kitchen door suddenly opened, flooding light into the hallway. Brewster turned and fired again, hitting the second man in the left cheek before he had a chance to take a shot. The body fell back and lay crumpled against the kitchen door. Brewster stayed in his crouched position, his gun covering the area in front of him. But there was no further commotion and the house quickly relapsed into silence. Brewster suddenly felt phlegm rising in his stomach and the blood pounding in his ears.

"Jean!" he shouted desperately up the stairs. And then he was racing up them. He reached the landing and started kicking in all the doors, his gun at the ready, poised to shoot down any other man who might be hiding there. But there was no-one. He reached the bedroom. The door was wide open. Brewster carefully peered round the door.

Jean was on the bed, propped up, like a giant stuffed doll. Otherwise, the room was empty. He stood framed in the doorway, numbness creeping up his body. Her large, dark brown eyes were wide open, her long jet-black hair hanging messily over her shoulders. She was wearing a simple, white dress, which had been ripped down the front. Bloody patches covered her entire body. She must have been dead for hours. And all on Caldwell's orders...

A creak sounded from the bathroom off to the left. The door was closed. Instantly, Brewster raised the gun and drilled three evenly spaced shots through it. Particles of wood blew up into the air and floated down to the carpet as the bullets struck. A loud thud could be heard from the other side of the door. Brewster carefully stepped across the room and opened it. The body, sagging under its own weight, had collapsed into the bath, the left leg inelegantly sprawled over the side, the right arm clawing at the tiles as if still desperately trying to cling onto life. Then it dropped down into the bath and was still. Brewster stepped into the bathroom and looked down at the body. The eyes of the killer stared away from him on to the empty, tiled bathroom wall, seeing nothing there. The killer's gun dropped into the bath. Two bloody patches spread across the man's shirt from where he had been hit in the stomach. The third bullet had clearly missed and embedded itself in the tiles. Brewster looked at the face, younger than his by several years, the look of shock now permanently etched onto it forever. These must have been out-of-towners, hired for the job. Brewster did not recognise the man. He pocketed his gun.

He walked back into the bedroom and stood at the end of the bed. Jean's empty eyes were staring right back at him; the eyes that had contained so much life and love for him before today; the eyes that no longer contained anything and never would again. Brewster sat down on the edge of the bed and examined her body. Both arms were dotted with angry, red cigarette burns. Both arms were tied to the ends of the bed head. There were red marks around her neck from where the men had strangled the life out of her. He dared not imagine what else they had done to her beforehand. She would have suffered terribly though. Brewster took her dead left hand and lifted it, stroking the cold fingers. He kissed them once. His eyes suddenly filled with tears, and he choked back the emotion. He leaned forward and gently closed the wide, staring eyes. Brewster then looked wildly around, shutting his emotions down, the waves of grief now giving way to the red-hot pokers of fury that lanced through him. One day, he promised himself, he would kill Caldwell. Then his instinctive discipline kicked in and he cleared his head. Right now, Caldwell would have to wait. There would be a contract out on him, and he needed to get out fast. He must disappear completely. He must, to all intents and purposes, be dead. He would need the £50,000 for himself now to accomplish this. He would have to use Tilbury Docks as a means of getting out of the country. There was of course at least a fifty per cent chance that they would work out that he would go there and would be waiting for him, but he had to take the gamble. It was the best chance he had. Hurriedly he grabbed the briefcase and raced for the bedroom door.

The black Mercedes appeared at the end of the street, its amber indicator light winking. It parked discreetly on the opposite side of the street, a few doors down from Jean's town house. The purring engine fell silent. The three shadowy figures in the car sat like statues, studying the house.   Up the street, the front door opened, and the elegant figure of John Brewster dashed out, looking all around as he did so, his hand clamped in his overcoat pocket.   And then, very quickly, his figure had vanished into the distance.   A second later, a taxi parked outside the house drove hurriedly away up the street.

In the driver's seat, Tom Noonan indicated down the street.   "Was that him?"

Seated in the passenger seat, Lomax nodded once.   "That was him. John Brewster."

In the back seat, Spanton asked, "So we pick him up, right?   Before he gets away?"

As if to answer his question, two black, menacing looking cars squealed into the road from the opposite end and screeched to a halt outside the town house.

Lomax's body imperceptibly stiffened.   "Hold it!" he ordered tersely. He watched carefully.   The car doors were flung open, forcibly ejecting six well built, sullen, fierce looking men on to the pavement. They were all wearing heavy overcoats and looked exactly like what they were: hired criminals of the most vicious variety. They crashed up the steps and smashed their way through the front door, into the house. "No, leave him. He's too hot right now. We need to do it when we have the upper hand. Spanton, you're with me." He turned to Noonan. "Noonan, you go and pick up Vogel. You've read the file?"

"All of it," confirmed Noonan, handing a brown paper file back to him. Lomax took it and placed it in the glove compartment.

"Then get on with it. We meet at the safehouse later. Spanton, you're driving."

Noonan opened the door and stepped on to the pavement. Spanton came round and took the driver's seat. Without a word, he gunned the engine, threw it into first gear, and the Mercedes roared off down the street. Noonan watched it for a moment and then turned, walking away in the opposite direction.

$\underline{4}$

Catherine Ferris had a new name and a new life – and suddenly found herself happy for the first time. She was renting a furnished, comfortable basement flat in Hammersmith, W6, where she lived alone, and had managed to secure herself a respectable job at London Library, where she worked as an assistant. Her work mainly involved issuing and returning books, dealing with fines, and generally assisting the library users with a wide range of requests. She had worked there for six months and was now completely settled in her role. And she enjoyed London too, the cool climate and peculiar but charming rituals.

She sat on her usual bench in St James Square, where she tended to spend her lunch hour, with the usual view of the equestrian statue of William III straight ahead of her. Pigeons fluttered at her feet. She stared at the statue and found herself daydreaming again. She wondered if she could ever be happy married to an Englishman. Sometimes she wished she could meet him. She was not lonely but had made no real friends in London.

She suddenly stubbed her cigarette out on the arm of the bench and glanced anxiously at her watch. It was two o' clock exactly! She would be late! Where did the time go? She snatched up her brown leather handbag, stood up and strode briskly back to the library, her high-heeled, knee-high brown leather boots snapping on the paving stones in strict rhythm, like a metronome.

Catherine Ferris was twenty-nine years old, a tall brunette, with striking brown eyes and a wide mouth. Too wide, she thought. She had always believed it was a rather unattractive mouth. Not that that seemed to matter these days. When she spoke, it was with a clipped, very precise, upper-class accent. Her colleagues in the library often teased her behind her back for her "posh" speaking voice. It never bothered her. She kept apart from them and cared nothing for what they thought of her. She usually dressed for work in sensible white blouses and grey, pleated skirts. She was statuesque at five foot nine and wore a pair of thick-framed, large spectacles. She always wore her hair tied severely back in a tight bun for work. This gave her an anonymous look, which she felt entirely comfortable with, given her unusual circumstances. Nonetheless, she was frequently aware of men glancing furtively and admiringly at her as she marched confidently past them around the city. It didn't bother her; in fact, she rather liked it. After work, she would let her hair down, shake it around, and put on a comfortable, baggy sweater. Glancing quickly from left to right, she hurried across St James's Square, her beige overcoat flapping in the winter breeze, and up the steps into the library.

At five thirty later that day, Catherine was walking past the receptionist.

"Good night, Catherine," she called out.

"Good night," Catherine replied. Her colleagues Trudie and Sandie left the building at the same time, scuttling away in the other direction towards Ryder Street, leaving Catherine to walk slowly away in the opposite direction, alone. It was getting dark. She reached the end of Charles II Street and was about to cross the main road into Soho when she saw something that almost made her pass out.

A thin man with wide, suspicious eyes, a long, pointed nose and a mouth that turned downwards was standing directly opposite her on the other side of the street staring right at her. He was dressed entirely in black, with a shiny black leather jacket buttoned up. His gaze seemed to penetrate her. He looked like a Gestapo interrogator. For a second, the world went silent. Catherine found herself locked into this terrible man's fixed gaze, unable to move. For the awful truth, she realised, was that she knew this man – and he knew her. His was a face from her old life. And he could destroy the new one that she had worked so hard to build up.

Catherine's face assumed a blank expression and she casually turned left up Waterloo Place, striding purposefully towards Soho. She must lose this man! Once she got to Soho, it would be easier to disappear into the narrow streets and large crowds. She tried not to appear in a hurry, and never once glanced back at the thin man. Yet she knew he was always there, following her on the other side of the street. All the time she felt his black shadow upon her. Keeping her head turned away, she hurried past Piccadilly tube station, turning right into Brewer Street, increasing her pace as she did so. And all the time, she felt the man sticking to her, felt his eyes drilling through the back of her head. Out of the corner of her eye, she sensed the man crossing to her side of the street and panic welled up in her stomach. The streets were getting busier now, the office leavers and theatregoers swarming all around her. Using them as cover, Catherine broke into a run, her heels slamming onto the pavement with loud cracks. She glanced twice at her watch, thinking herself into the role of a theatregoer who was running late. She reached Wardour Street and glanced for a second to her left. A taxi was bearing down on her, but she took the gamble and dived across the street. She felt the taxi looming over her, but she made it safely to the pavement on the other side. The taxi primly sounded its horn in protest but was quickly gone. A steady stream of traffic followed it, making it impossible for the man to follow her across the street. Catherine raced to the end of the road and turned left into Shaftesbury Avenue.

She desperately wanted to get home quickly but was suddenly aware of how hungry she had become. She would find a quiet café, eat something, and then get home.

The café was in Holborn. It had taken her twenty minutes to walk there, and she felt it was safely out of the way. She found a booth and sat down, facing the door but covered by a partition. An Indian waiter approached her, and she ordered a chicken sandwich and a black coffee. They arrived five minutes later, and she gratefully devoured the sandwich.

Suddenly in front of her, a man was sitting down opposite her, invading her booth. She looked up, startled and suddenly angry. But the man was a stranger, with a pudgy face, and mean, greedy little eyes. His hair was lank and turning grey. He wore an old suit under his mackintosh and his plump stomach jutted into the side of the table. To Catherine, he was a revolting creature, but she felt in no danger from him. She understood exactly what he was about though; he was a hardened city worker, a successful man, wealthy, probably married, maybe even a QC, who was chancing his luck with her, most likely for his own amusement.

"Mind if I join you?" he asked in a brash, confident tone.

But then another voice broke in, just behind Catherine. "I rather think she might, yes." The stranger looked up. Catherine turned and followed his gaze. A second stranger stood there, staring down the pudgy man. He had thick, chestnut hair, quite long and slightly curly. His eyes were clear grey, from which emanated a warmth and kindness that was nowhere to be found on the rest of his hard, chiselled face. The voice did not fit the face or lean body though; it was a quiet, sensitive voice, more in keeping with a college professor. Catherine was confused by the man, unsure whether she should feel afraid of him or not. "Now, if you don't mind, I'd like to talk to my wife. Goodbye."

The intruder got the message straight away, turned and walked to the door.

"Bastard!" he called out contemptuously as he threw the door open, letting in a blast of cold air, and stepped out into the darkening evening. All was quiet in the café again.

The stranger smiled down at Catherine.

"Well, I'm very glad to meet you at last – Katharina Vogel."

Catherine felt a shockwave shoot up her stomach. She searched the stranger's face for answers, but she found none. She would play the role that she had carefully created for herself right through to the end.

"Who are you?"

"My name is Tom Noonan."

"Well, my name is Catherine Ferris," she insisted in her precise, upper-class voice. "I work at London Library. I have never heard of Katharina..."

"You're wasting time, Katharina. And time is something you're quickly running out of. You've got maybe five minutes." Noonan smiled for the first time. "Your real name is Katharina Vogel. You were born in Bregenz, Austria, December 3rd, 1943. Your father was a university lecturer, your mother a concert pianist. You were born into a life of wealth and privilege – until you started to go wrong. You became a member of the Richter-Hoffman terrorist cell in West Germany. You're wanted by the West German police for murder, hijacking, and arson. The rest of your outfit were rounded up after the Frankfurt Airport debacle. Three were shot by police, the others are all in prison. But you escaped, the only one who did. Or so you thought. You came to this country six months ago and thought you'd made a clean getaway. But this evening you found out that Hans Bruchner is also free. He escaped from prison a month ago and came over here to look for you. The word is that you sold out the rest of the group to the authorities in return for a safe passage here."

Katharina stared back at him, still determined to play her role of Catherine Ferris right to the end.

"I still have no idea what you're talking about," she replied. "I think you must be crazy or something." She paused, letting her breath slowly out through close lips. "You said something about my having only five minutes?" she asked.

Noonan nodded. "You lost Bruchner at Shaftesbury Avenue. Unfortunately for you though he picked up your tail again at Macklin Street. But you're good and you managed to lose him again. Right now, he knows you're in Holborn somewhere and he'll be checking all the cafés. He'll get to this one soon enough."

"Assuming this is true, how would you know this?" she asked.

"Because I was following Bruchner while he was following you," replied Noonan. "I can take you to a safe place."

But Katharina's face had turned away from Noonan's and was looking down the café at the door which had suddenly opened again. Noonan had felt the cool breeze on the back of his head. Katharina's expression was suddenly pensive, frightened.

"There's no time left," Katharina told Noonan matter-of-factly. "He's already here."

Hans Bruchner, his wide eyes glowing with triumph, and his mouth curled up in a victorious sneer, had just entered the café and had spotted Katharina immediately. He just stood there, propped up against the door, blocking the way out, looking straight at Katharina, a horrible smile on his face.

Noonan did not look.

"Well, it's a simple choice you have, isn't it?" he told her.

5

Katharina's mind was already made up. She stood and looked at him expectantly. For the first time, she took in his clothes. He was wearing a black polo-neck sweater under a dark blue naval overcoat, which seemed an odd choice of garment. Noonan took her arm and guided her towards the door. Bruchner's faced loomed at them as they approached the door and a hideous gloat spread across it. He straightened his body, and his right hand went further into his jacket pocket.

"Katharina - where are you going?" he taunted her in an awful, sing-song voice.

"Ignore him," Noonan whispered into her ear. They stepped up to him. "Excuse me, please," he spoke to Bruchner, looking him directly in the eye.

"She hasn't even introduced us yet, and you're already wanting to go. That's not polite," Bruchner sneered.

"Well, let me put it another way, then," Noonan replied. And with that, his right arm suddenly shot out like a piston, his fist connecting hard with Bruchner's ribcage. Bruchher grunted in pain and his body slid to the floor. A voice yelled out behind them. Quickly Noonan kicked Bruchner's body out of the way, opened the door and bundled Katharina through it. "Quick! We must lose him," he told her urgently.

They half-ran to the end of Red Lion Street. All the time, they could hear Bruchner, who had seemingly recovered quickly and was already after them, calling out to them, taunting them in a heavily accented voice.

"Katharina," he crowed to her. "Why do you run from me?" Then, in a harder voice, "I'm going to kill you, you bastard!"

"Just keep moving," Noonan told her quietly. They could hear his loud footsteps on the wet pavement as he ran after them. They turned left onto the busy

A40.   A couple of stray taxis and lorries swished past, but there were few other pedestrians.   Katharina stayed close on Noonan's tail.

Up ahead they could see the familiar, illuminated, red, white, and blue underground sign for Chancery Road tube station, the only warm and comforting sight in what was turning out to be a dark, bleak, and drizzly evening.

"Make for the tube station," Noonan ordered her.   They picked up their pace and started running hard.   Behind them, Bruchner also broke into a run.   Katharina found it hard running in her leather boots and her pace started to flag.   Noonan looked around for her, grabbed her hand wildly and pulled her along.

They made it to the sign and raced down the steps into the underground.   At the bottom of the steps, they ran noisily down the tunnel.   A ticket vendor sitting at a window, leaned forward, and yelled something at them.

The bright, white tiled passageway coiled around ahead of them.   The loud snaps of Bruchner's rapid footsteps echoed all around them.   The passageway opened and the escalators appeared ahead of them. Noonan and Katharina flew down the descending escalator on the left-hand side, clumsily knocking into two late night travellers who were lined up to the left. The second, a Jamaican man, called out something to them that Katharina could not understand. At the bottom they followed another twisting tunnel that took them out to Platform One of the Central Line. They ran to the far end of the platform and turned back, their breath coming out in sharp gasps.

Behind them, Bruchner's black leather-jacketed figure quickly emerged from the tunnel and onto the platform. He saw them, smiled, and shook his head. There were two other passengers sitting on benches, waiting to board the next incoming train.

"Don't worry, he won't try anything here, not with witnesses around," Noonan told Katharina. Soon the rumble of the next train could he heard and felt, its grey snout quickly edging its way out of the darkness of the tunnel. It crashed through into the station and stopped with a heaving sigh. The two late night passengers automatically stood up and waited for the doors to hiss open. Bruchner glanced anxiously at the grey train and then back at Noonan and Katharina. He tried to read their thoughts. Noonan stood facing Bruchner, holding Katharina's hand tightly. Brucher's body was coiled, ready to pounce. But Noonan held his position. The doors opened and a group of three males spilled out onto the platform, the fragments of their conversation disappearing into the station as they vanished up the tunnel. Noonan glanced at the train, its open doors beckoning them in. Bruchner's eyes flashed wildly at them, perspiration breaking out across his forehead. The doors started to hiss shut.

Noonan suddenly exploded into action, pulling Katharina towards the train. Bruchner moved simultaneously and all three bounded onto the train. Then just as the doors were about to seal shut, Noonan shoved his shoe out, the doors catching it and wheezing open again. Noonan pulled Katharina out again onto the platform. The train started to pull away, but Bruchner had managed to break out onto the platform too, a victorious leer on his face. The train heaved away and crashed into the tunnel, heading eastwards, its sound disappearing into the bowels of the earth.

They were now alone on the platform. It was quarter to seven. Bruchner had the exit covered. Noonan looked up and down the platform and made an immediate decision. He pulled Katharina back to the end of the platform. She gave a gasp as he pulled her down the slope and into the impenetrable blackness of the underground tunnel. They were quickly enveloped entirely by the black void. Behind her Katharina could hear Bruchner following them down into the tunnel. She turned and saw his silhouette against the distant light, then nothing. She could feel the wall of the tunnel brushing against her right shoulder and tried to hug it as much as possible. She could hear Noonan ahead but not see him. Then the tunnel opened out slightly. She felt Noonan pull her into a black space to the right, but her vision and sense of direction had completely gone now. She no longer knew which way was forward or back and could see nothing. She could only feel the man Noonan pulling her towards him and holding her still.

"Shh!" he hissed briefly, urgently into her ear.

They stayed like that for what seemed like three minutes. She could hear Bruchner's faltering footsteps approaching from somewhere to the left, but they sounded tentative. She heard a distinct click, which may have been a switchblade or a handgun. She held her breath. Then there came the familiar rumbling sound of another train coming from the same direction as the previous one. A distant light started to fill the tunnel, which grew in intensity. The ghastly figure of Bruchner, standing directly in front of them with his back to them, was steadily becoming illuminated by the light from the oncoming train. He had a switchblade in his right hand, which he was holding outwards like a sword. He was about three feet away. All he had to do was turn around and he would see them! As if reading her thoughts, Bruchner's body started to turn.

Noonan then exploded into action, leaping forward. Katharina followed and leapt forward after him. Bruchner's eyes suddenly blazed at them, and he flashed the knife viciously out at Noonan.

Katharina kicked out desperately at Bruchner's right kneecap, the sharp heel of her heavy leather book slamming into it. There was a sharp crack, followed by a scream from Bruchner. His body collapsed to the ground. Katharina grabbed his wrist and twisted it ferociously. The knife clattered harmlessly to the ground. Noonan threw himself quickly on top of Bruchner and, clamping his arms to the ground with his knees, repeatedly struck out at his trachea with the sharp edge of his flattened hand. A horrible gurgling sound came from Bruchner's throat, his teeth bared in a ghastly grimace of death. His eyes briefly flashed with the final realisation, before all life was finally extinguished from them, and they dulled over. A second later, the train crashed round the corner, flooding the tunnel with light. Katharina could see finally that they were in a small alcove in the wall. Had they not made it there, the train would certainly have crushed them to death. Katharina and Noonan lay on top of Bruchner's dead body, their breathing coming out in painful gasps. Noonan looked down one last time at Bruchner's face. Noonan closed his eyes, shutting the memory out. Above them, the lights from the windows of the rushing tube train flashed all around them like a crazy light show. Then they were suddenly plunged into darkness again and the train was rolling away, gurgling into the darkest recesses of the tunnel. Then all was silent.

Noonan picked Katharina up from the ground. They looked at each other for a moment, sharing the immense weight of what had just happened to them. Then, without saying a word to each other, they were moving quickly again, back towards the distant light of the platform, back towards the warm, comfortable land of the living.

6

The safehouse was above a row of shops outside Russell Square. In keeping with its purpose, it was as remarkably unremarkable a flat as one could imagine. Apart from a fish and chips shop, which was just closing for the night, the remaining shop fronts were silent black squares. Noonan and Katharina hurriedly crossed the road from Russell Square tube station and made it to the front door. Noonan unlocked the expensive wooden door and let Katharina in, closing the door behind him. A staircase led up to a front door on the first floor. Noonan unlocked this and showed Katharina in. She slipped inside and he turned on the light.

Katharina walked ahead down a sparse, echoey hallway, that led through to an expansive living room with white walls

71

and a green carpet. There was a perfunctory settee, a round table, and that was about it. A kitchen area could be seen through an open door to the side and two other doors were over in the far wall. It looked like a flat that had recently been vacated, waiting for the new residents to move in. Even the walls seemed to have been stripped of paint. Noonan locked the front door and joined Katharina in the living room.

"What is this place?" she asked.

"Safehouse," Noonan replied.

"You were going to tell me who you work for?"

"You've been recruited by a man called Lomax," Noonan told her.

"Lomax?" She processed the name, but it registered nothing.

"Lomax's division deals with internal security threats to the United Kingdom, tackling the sort of jobs that MI6 and the Special Branch want nothing to do with," explained Noonan.

"And if I refuse to co-operate?"

"Then you'll be handed over to Scotland Yard's Special Branch, who will then hand you over to the West German police. You'll serve a life sentence in a German prison for murder. Co-operate on the other hand and Lomax will arrange for you to disappear again after the job."

Katharina's voice hardened and her German accent became more pronounced. "But I've committed no crimes in this country."

"It doesn't matter," countered Noonan. "Lomax will have you shipped straight back to West Germany. They've had a warrant out for you for six months. What was it? Nine civilians killed in the Frankfurt bombing; at least two bank robberies that can be put down to your outfit. Two security guards shot and killed…"

"I was only the getaway driver on those jobs," Katharina insisted forcefully.

"You were identified inside at least one of the banks by eyewitnesses," Noonan countered. "And the bomb that was used at Frankfurt was yours. You made it. Did you know that two of the dead were only children?"

"My people are at war," Katharina shot back. "In war people die. And I don't have to listen to any more of this!"

With that, Katharina turned away and strode angrily back down the hallway. She snatched at the front door handle and turned it. She knew it was a futile gesture, but it momentarily made her feel better. She leaned defeatedly against the door. Noonan was standing at the far end of the hallway looking at her thoughtfully.

"Locked," he said without emotion. "There's nowhere to go." He walked up to her and gently took her arm. He then smiled unexpectedly. She walked resignedly back into the living room.

"Sit down." Noonan gestured towards the tea-stained white sofa.

Katharina did so, sighing wearily. She closed her eyes for a second, then opened them again, looking at Noonan.

"What right do you have to judge me?" she asked him wearily.

"I'm not judging you," he answered softly.

She turned away. Noonan took a step towards her, and the questions started again. "So, when you came over here, what was your plan?"

"I'd had enough," Katharina answered. "I'm not sorry for any of the things that we did, I still believe we were justified. It's just that nothing was changing; we weren't getting anywhere."

"And that's when you created Catherine Ferris and tried to start again?"

She nodded and yawned, realising then how tired she was. It had been a long day and she was out of answers now.

"When was the last time you saw Jurgen Richter?" Noonan continued.

"I haven't seen him since his arrest two years ago. He means nothing to me anymore."

"He was your lover," Noonan replied. "You had a child together, a boy. Christian. He's living with your mother now..."

At the mention of her son, Katharina suddenly leaned forward and erupted furiously, "How would you like to go and...?"

"Alright, forget it," Noonan brusquely jumped in, holding up his hand. Katharina stopped, her face reddening. Then she exhaled sharply and sat back on the sofa. She eyed him coldly. "So, you see, Miss Vogel," continued Noonan, "there's not much that Lomax doesn't know about you."

"Well, to hell with you and to hell with Lomax," Katharina replied with a quiet anger. "How long do we have to stay here?"

"Until Lomax gets here," replied Noonan. "That could be later tonight."

"I've got no other clothes to wear," she sighed wearily.

"All your clothes were brought over from your flat in Hammersmith this afternoon. They're in the wardrobe in your bedroom."

Her eyes followed Noonan as he walked to the first of the bedroom doors. He opened it as though showing off the master bedroom.

"This is yours," he told her.

She got up and walked into the bedroom. It was as spartan as the rest of the flat, almost like a cell. There was a window above a double bed. She looked up at it.

"It's alarmed," Noonan warned her. Katharina noticed a white cable running along the bottom of the windowsill. She went to the cupboard, opened it, and saw the clothes from her flat hanging there neatly. She took her overcoat off and threw it on the bed. She stood facing Noonan in her white blouse and grey skirt. She reached up and untied her hair, shaking it out. She finished by taking her glasses off. She suddenly looked five years younger and much more attractive. Her hair was thick and silky and fell down her back.

"How long will it take for them to find the body?" she asked.

"A few days," he replied. "But we're in the clear. There's nothing to connect it with us."

She sat down on the bed and looked away, tired. Finally, she said, "I thought I'd finally got out."

"People like us never get out. Believe me, I know," Noonan replied. "You'd better get some sleep. I'll be next door." Noonan turned to leave. Before closing the door, he turned to her one last time. "Goodnight, Miss Vogel."

"Goodnight, Mr er…"

"Noonan," he reminded her.

She turned away glumly as Noonan closed the door. She looked around the room. The window was slim and rectangular. It would have been locked as well as alarmed. The only other way out was the front door, and that she had already tried. She was locked in with the man Noonan, and she would just have to get used to it for the time being.

She unbuttoned her blouse and unzipped her skirt and leather boots. Then she suddenly stopped and wondered if there was a camera in the room. She looked warily around the walls and the ceiling but saw nothing that looked like one. If it was there, it was well hidden.

Katharina dismissed the idea from her mind; she was not ashamed of her body. She took a couple of hangers from the cupboard and hung up her blouse and skirt. She found her white pyjama top in one of the drawers. Whoever had cleaned out her flat had certainly done a thorough job. She always wore just the pyjama top, leaving her legs free. There was a small sink in the corner of the room, with a toothbrush and paste in a small glass. She used these to brush her teeth, watching her tired, nervous face in the mirror as she did so. Then she walked to the light switch and turned it off.

She moved gracefully through the darkness and slipped gratefully under the continental quilt, which felt soft and luxurious on her skin. She stared up at the black ceiling and pondered the man Noonan. Everything about his manner and body language marked him out as a cold, hard professional espionage man. And yet...

Whatever this assignment was though, she would have to see it through. The idea of a life sentence in a German prison she could not face. Brigitta Hoffman had been found hanging in her cell three months into her sentence. The coroner had entered a verdict of suicide, but was that really the truth? The case had made the papers, even the British ones. And what guarantees did she have? They could very easily hand her over to the West German police after the job anyway. She would have to do whatever was necessary, and kill whoever she had to, to stay free. She may even have to kill the man Noonan. She knew she would not hesitate, if it came to it. In similar cases, she had never hesitated before. This disconcerting tangle of anxieties tumbled relentlessly across her mind until eventually sleep mercifully embraced her.

7

In the next room, Noonan sat back and stared at the wall, beyond which Katharina was willing sleep to take her away. Like Katharina's room, Noonan's looked and felt like a prison cell. There was a bed, a cupboard, bare walls and not much else. The room, if he had thought about it, reflected what his life had turned into.

But he did find himself thinking about the girl in the next room. Had he been convinced by her story? The words and sentiment had been delivered with conviction, but the eyes had remained hard and cold, unrepentant to the last. He had met many women like her, and they had all shared the same empty look in their eyes; all in all, he decided, Katharina Vogel, or Catherine Ferris, or whatever she liked to call herself, was a duplicitous, scheming woman who had somehow escaped the justice that was surely owed to her. He knew that she would kill him without a moment's hesitation, and he must be prepared to do the same to her. He found the idea of working with a wanted terrorist thoroughly objectionable, but he had been ordered to by Lomax, and for now there was nothing he could do about it. He pondered on Alan Spanton, who he had been with for three days now. He was exactly the type that Lomax would go for: highly trained, anti-social and deeply dysfunctional. He was always aware of the man's eyes boring resentfully into his and sensed his natural antagonism and paranoia towards him. Spanton had seemed to feel threatened by Noonan's presence right from the start and would no doubt want to prove his physical superiority against him sooner or later. The fourth member of the new team, John Brewster, remained a mystery. What kind of a man would he turn out to be? And just what kind of a job was Lomax preparing?

And then there had been the man in the underground. It had been many years since Noonan had had to kill a man with his bare hands, and the experience had shaken him badly. None of this would have been apparent to the girl, however. He had been trained to hide those feelings, but right now, in this room, Noonan felt his right hand shaking slightly. In this room, his private cell, there were no secrets. It had been a personal, ugly killing. Noonan felt no remorse about the man's death; many innocent people had died at his hands and many more would have had he been allowed to live. He had been the very worst kind of man, but the terrified eyes at the point of death had pleaded with him. And it was those eyes that came back to haunt him now. He had seen them many times over the course of his life. He never forgot the eyes.

And then suddenly he was seeing again the dying eyes of the deadliest man he had ever encountered – Jimmy Jarrett. His eyes had been different from all the others though. There had been no fear in them. Instead, they had held a personal message for him. They seemed to tell him that he would see him again in the next life. Thoughts of Jarrett brought him back to the month of October, the most magical of his life, when he had met Anna Raven, the beautiful, fearless girl whose life he had saved in North Devon, and who had later saved his in return. Jarrett had hunted them relentlessly for several days and during that time they had fallen deeply in love with each other. Curiously though, Jarrett had become as much a part of that magical month as Anna because the two of them, he had realised over the last four months, had come to personify the two conflicting sides of his own personality.

Noonan had always suffered from nightmares. He used to have them about Lomax, but now it was Jarrett who would come to haunt him in his sleep. It was the same nightmare most nights: Noonan would travel back to Mr Burton's farm, where he had killed and buried Jarrett, to make sure that his grave was still intact; and every time, there would be a hole in the ground where Jarrett's body should have been. He had somehow managed to crawl out of his grave and was out there, killing again. He understood what the nightmare meant: Jarrett was dead – but for Noonan, he never would be.

And then there was Anna, the only woman in his life he had ever loved. She had given him hope and the promise of a bright and peaceful future. She had saved his life in more ways than one. Up until Anna, his life had been an unsettled, and unhappy one, full of darkness and death.

Noonan had travelled back to the cottage he had shared with Anna in the Cotswolds but had found it empty. He had asked around the various locals but had been treated with hostility and suspicion. They simply told him that Anna was gone – and no, they had no idea of her whereabouts. Then the doors had slammed in his face. And then Lomax had made him aware that he was holding Anna somewhere and would kill her if Noonan did not co-operate with him. Then there had been Tristan, his best friend, who had travelled down to help them escape from Jarrett. But he could not think about Tristan right now. It simply upset him too much...

Noonan always managed to keep Anna out of his thoughts during the day, but at night he would think only of her as he lay there in the darkness, remembering the delicate brush of her body against his as they had made love, her soft sighs as he had rolled her over and kissed all round her body. He always hugged his pillow at night, imagining it was her body lying next to his.

Noonan opened his wallet and took out the small black and white photograph that was always the last thing he looked at before he turned the light out. The photograph was of Anna, sitting on the edge of a Wayfarer dinghy with the open channel and white skies stretching out behind her. Anna loved the water. The monochrome image strongly accentuated her aristocratic beauty and strong, leonine features. Her auburn hair flowed out in thick waves. Her arms were gripping the edge of the boat as though it was being strongly rocked about in the wind. She was wearing a thick white sweater. She was smiling, but it was a sad and wistful smile, as though she already knew at the height of those happiest of days that their happiness would soon have to come to an end.

Noonan put the photograph to his lips and kissed it gently, as he did every night. Then he replaced it in his wallet, reached over and turned his bedside light out.   He held the memory of Anna's face tightly to him as he closed his eyes and tried to drift off into an untroubled sleep.

8

Noonan's eyes snapped open, and his mind was suddenly alert. What was it? The sense of extreme and very real danger close by was palpable and he felt his stomach churning. There was somebody in his room! But who? Very slowly, his arm reached out for the lamp at his bedside. He tensed his body and snapped the switch on. As light flooded the room, he prepared to fling his body forward towards his assailant. Lomax was smiling down at him sadistically, leaning against the door. He was dressed in an expensive black overcoat and a pair of leather gloves, looking watchful and alert, as always. In his hand was a brown leather briefcase.

"Good morning." Lomax's voice was a velvet sneer. Noonan blinked once, clearing the sleepiness from his eyes, the harsh light still stabbing into them. Slowly they adjusted themselves. He wanted to hurl abuse at Lomax, but any words failed to materialise. "Get dressed," he ordered, his voice now suddenly brusque and business-like. "We've found Brewster. He'll be at Tilbury Docks at 2.30, so we need to move fast. The contract on him has doubled." With that, Lomax turned and left the room.

Noonan squinted at the watch at the side of his bed. It was five minutes to one. He had been asleep for less than three hours. He forced himself out of bed, silently cursing Lomax, and started to dress. Two minutes later he was in the living room.

Lomax was waiting for him, Spanton standing slightly behind him, wearing a black leather jacket over a grey polo neck and a pair of brown corduroys. His curly blond hair was brushed back from his forehead, and he was clean shaven. His bright green eyes sparkled fiercely and resentfully at Noonan. Despite the early hour, he looked wide awake.

"Go and wake Miss Vogel, Noonan," Lomax ordered him, clearly enjoying the power he held over him. Noonan noticed a twitch of a smile forming on Spanton's lips as the order came out. Noonan stepped over to Katharina's room and hammered his fist on the door. He waited a few seconds and hammered again. This time the door opened, and Katharina peered sleepily and angrily out at him.

"It's time to get up. Lomax is here," he told her. Katharina replied with a filthy two-word epithet and slammed the door in his face. They waited, standing in a circle in the living room, eyeing each other warily. It was Lomax who finally spoke.

"I'm surprised at you, Spanton," he said, looking directly at Noonan. "You've been around Noonan for three days now. And in all that time you've never tried to take him." Noonan looked over to Spanton who was glowering redly at him. "Well, I wouldn't try it if I were you," continued Lomax calmly. "Noonan outclasses you. I trained him. You'll find out soon enough."

At this, Spanton's face noticeably darkened further.

"Better watch yourself around him, Noonan," Lomax smiled, enjoying his sadistic game. "I think he's taken a bit of a shine to you." As always, his presence and natural sense of authority were so palpable that Noonan could feel an electrical charge in the room. Spanton took a couple of steps towards Noonan, his eyes boring into him, itching for him to make a move. But Noonan held his ground.

The moment was broken by the sound of Katharina's bedroom door opening. She stepped out, dressed simply in dark blue jeans and a dark khaki sweater. She wore no makeup.

"Katharina Vogel," Lomax told Spanton. Katharina shot him a wary glance. "I wouldn't advise either of you turning your backs on her. She's more ruthless than either of you."

Katharina eyed him coldly. "You're Lomax?" There was poison in her voice.

Lomax did not answer her. Instead, he moved swiftly over to the table, his movements economical and precise. He opened his briefcase and looked up at all three of them. "Let's get one thing straight. You are all working for me, and we all have a job to do. It starts now. Try to run and I'll kill you."

"What's the job?" Spanton asked.

Lomax gave him a look that sent a chill across the room. "Later," he simply replied. Lomax glared at Spanton for a second before he resumed. "First of all, we go to pick up Brewster. He'll be working with us." Lomax paused and watched the faces of the other three. Katharina's face registered nothing, but he could detect apprehension in the faces of the other two. "Of course, he may not feel like coming with us, in which case we'll have to persuade him."

Lomax reached into the briefcase and took out a Browning Hi-Power automatic pistol. He held it up for the other three. "You'll get them later. There may be shooting." Then Lomax leaned forward, his palms flat on the table, his eyes glittering fiercely again. "If you try to use those to escape from me, then you won't live beyond this evening." He dropped the gun back into the briefcase and snapped the leather flap down over the lock. "Time to go."

At quarter past two that morning, they were sitting in Lomax's black Mercedes, parked in a corner of the warehouse leading out to Tilbury Docks. They had arrived an hour earlier, having driven hard across town to make it ahead of schedule. Noonan had been driving, and just out of personal spite had driven with a wild, reckless abandon, taking corners too fast and weaving dangerously in and out of the odd car that was still on the road at this early hour. He had wanted to see if he could shake up Lomax sitting in the back seat. No chance. Lomax had remained calm, oblivious even. If you pushed him over a ravine in a go-kart, he would still fail to break a sweat. Even Katharina, in the passenger seat, had occasionally glanced at him nervously. Now, in the warehouse, the car was well hidden, parked in the shadows in a far corner behind a stack of cardboard boxes. Noonan remained in the driver's seat with Katharina sitting next to him. Lomax sat in the back on the right, where he could keep a close eye on everyone, with Spanton next to him, two black shapes obscured by the darkness. Katharina was now wearing a tan coloured, belted suede short trench coat, which she had buttoned up to the neck to protect her from the biting cold. Noonan wore his naval overcoat. It was so cold that they were breathing out steam. The only light came from the floodlights on the dock. Noonan wiped the steamed-up windscreen with his fist.

Lomax peered at his watch in the darkness. "Right, it's time," he said. He leaned forward and picked up the briefcase. He opened it, handing the Browning automatics to Noonan and Spanton. He took out the third, leaned forward and held it out for Katharina. She just turned and stared back at him.

"Take it!" Lomax hissed. She coolly reached over and took the gun, laying it across her lap and feeling the cold, black metal on her fingertips. Noonan immediately pocketed his without looking at it. Only Spanton bothered to release the clip and check it, slamming it back home with more force than was necessary. Lomax and Noonan turned in their seats and eyed him coldly. Spanton, ignoring them, tucked the gun into his corduroys.

"Do you think he's here?" Noonan asked.

"He's here," Lomax confirmed. "Let's go and get him. And keep it quiet!" Lomax opened his car door softly and stepped out. The others followed his lead, shutting their car doors with a barely perceptible click. They moved quietly through the darkness towards the rectangle of light that led out to the docks. Katharina tucked her gun into the back of her jeans. Only Lomax moved forward with his gun at the ready. They fanned out in a semi-circle, Lomax in the middle. They stepped through the rectangular door and out onto the docks.

The long tarmac strip stretched ahead of them down towards the black water, the area lit by two sets of raised floodlights. Two giant cranes stood on either side like huge, silent sentries. Vast, steel containers were dotted along the strip, inappropriately bright in their garish colours, bright red and blue, emphasising the ugliness of the dismal industrial landscape. A forklift truck was moving around to the left. Otherwise, there were no signs of activity. The four walked slowly down the strip, Lomax a few feet in front. Katharina balled her fingers into fists and thrust them deep into her jacket pockets, trying to keep the cold out. She shivered involuntarily, aware that it was not just the cold that was getting to her. Noonan and Spanton also kept their hands in their pockets, staring grimly ahead of them. They peered into every nook and cranny, finding nothing there but black, innocent, empty space. If Brewster was close by, Noonan reflected sourly, he was keeping himself well hidden. Out in front, only Lomax appeared placid and relaxed. It took two minutes for the four of them to reach the water, and still there was no sign of Brewster.

"Take cover – now," Lomax suddenly ordered. Noonan moved quickly to the right, positioning himself behind one of the containers. Spanton moved to the left. Katharina found herself going with Noonan and positioning herself behind him. Lomax, alone on the strip, looked around him.

"Brewster!" he called out. There was no response. "Listen to me, Brewster. My name is Lomax. I know all about you, Brewster. I know you can hear me. There's something you need to know – your

96

people are on their way here to kill you! They could be here any minute. You need to come with me now!"

Lomax looked around. All he could hear was the distant rumble of the forklift truck. Nothing else moved and there was no other sound.

"Brewster?" he called out again, louder. "Time's running out! There's no way out of here unless you come with me!" Lomax felt a flicker of movement behind him and started to turn but it was too late. He felt the muzzle of an automatic pressing hard into the back of his skull. The man had come silently and invisibly out of the darkness, taking him from behind. Lomax was impressed.

"Take it easy, son," Lomax said quietly.

"Don't say another word." The voice had a trace of South London and was quietly warning him from the darkness. "Just stand still and don't move, otherwise you're a dead man."

"Brewster?"

"What do you want with me?"

"I want you alive."

"Why?"

"Because I need you that way."

There was silence for a moment and Lomax could sense the man processing this. Then the voice came back again. The threat behind it had eased slightly, but the force behind the hand holding the gun most certainly had not.

"How many men have you got?"

"Three."

"OK – why should I believe you, Lomax?"

"Well, it's a choice you've got to make, isn't it? What do *you* believe?"

Noonan peered out of the darkness. He could hear two voices talking softly: Lomax's and the voice of another man. He could not clearly see the other man though. Then Noonan saw something that almost stopped his breath. In the space of less than a second, Lomax had pirouetted on one foot, grabbed the other man's gun with one hand and the man's neck with the other. He heard a squawk of surprise and sudden intense pain from the other man. Noonan was forced to reflect once again that despite the loathing he felt for Lomax, his unarmed combat skills were almost supernatural. He was the most brilliant, capable agent he had ever known. But if there was a barely visible line between being a brilliant field agent and a certifiable maniac, then Lomax certainly had both feet on either side of it. In fact, Noonan had come to believe that they amounted to the same thing anyway.

"You're good, son," Lomax told Brewster admiringly. "But you could still learn a few things." He let go of Brewster's neck and turned to face him. Brewster was rubbing his sore neck and looking suspiciously back at Lomax. Lomax handed Brewster's gun back to him.

"Alright, just for the moment, let's say I'll buy it," said Brewster carefully, glancing at his gun. "What have you got in mind?"

"Not here," replied Lomax. "We'll get out of here first, then I'll tell you."

Brewster was distracted by the sight of two pairs of headlights coming towards them down the tarmac strip.

"It may be too late already," Brewster muttered bitterly into the chilly wind.

"Wait for my signal," Lomax ordered him.

The two cars rumbled menacingly towards them, holding them in the twin glares of their headlights. They were two dark coloured Ford Cortina mark IIIs. They pulled up alongside each other, blocking the way back to the warehouse. Behind them was the water. Lomax and Brewster were trapped, caught in the blinding headlights. The doors of the cars opened, and Lomax counted six shadows pouring out of the cars. They approached, and Lomax was soon able to make out the Colt Government pistols clamped in the black gloved hands and the hard, vicious eyes behind them. All six were wearing heavy black overcoats and at least half of them were wearing caps, keeping their faces in shadow. Lomax recognised them as the same crew that he had seen outside the Hampstead townhouse.

Behind the container, Noonan automatically felt his hand go for the .9mm in his pocket and he pulled it out. Without quite realising it, Katharina had instinctively followed his lead and the gun was already in her hand. Noonan turned to face her. He could sense the fear in her eyes, which matched his own. The fear always seized him at times like these. The shooting part was bad enough, but the build-up was always worse. One thing that Noonan could always be certain of though: Lomax would not be afraid. On the contrary, he would be enjoying himself right now. He told Katharina with his eyes to follow his lead – they would both be alright. He knew from her eyes that she had got the message and had understood.

The six men stood evenly apart, facing Lomax and Brewster. Lomax had positioned himself partially in front of Brewster, partly to protect him and partly so that he could focus completely on the men in front of them. The tallest one in the middle, who also appeared to be the most senior, stepped up to Lomax. The other five maintained their positions.

"Who are you?" he asked in a thick, working-class London accent.

"My name's Lomax. And Mr Brewster is coming with me."

"I don't think so, pal," replied the gruff voice. "We want Brewster. And seeing as you're in the way, it's going to have to be bye-bye for you as well. Sorry, pal."

"I'm not alone though," replied Lomax, in a raised voice.

Noonan recognised his cue and moved instantly. He had not worked for Lomax for five reluctant, miserable years without knowing the way his mind worked. Behind him, he could feel Katharina moving with him and, out of the corner of his eyes, he could see Spanton coming out of the darkness from the other side. Noonan had examined the situation from the darkness. Brewster and Lomax were in a central position, so they would take care of the middle two. He and Katharina would concentrate on the two on the far right, leaving Spanton to deal with the two on the far left. He gestured to Spanton to stay to the left and he nodded.

"I suggest you gentlemen lay those weapons on the ground," Lomax suggested in a reasonable voice.

For a second, there was no movement. Noonan could just see the backs of the six men tensed and coiled. He had the back of the second man from the right firmly in his sight. He hoped desperately he would not have to squeeze the trigger. Then, as if they had communicated by telepathy, all six turned as one. Noonan fired automatically and he heard Katharina and Spanton firing a split second after him. The three men in their sights dropped to the ground. Behind the falling men, Noonan saw in a blur of movement Lomax pulling Brewster to the ground as two shots sang out over their heads. Both Lomax and Brewster fired simultaneously from the ground and the two men in the middle, one of them the leader, collapsed on top of their fallen comrades. But then Noonan saw the sixth man, the one on the far left, running behind one of the containers.

"Spanton! To your left!" shouted Noonan. Spanton nodded and they both raced into the shadows. At the edge of his consciousness, Noonan became aware that the sound of the forklift truck had cut out. The operator, having heard the shooting, was clearly running terrified for the nearest telephone to dial three nines. As well he should, the poor bastard. He was probably just some average plodder working some overtime to bring back something nice for his wife. To get into the middle of a dockland shootout with a bunch of lunatics was the last thing he would have been banking on. Well, they had better get this finished quickly then, otherwise Lomax would be answering some embarrassing questions from the police. Noonan crept around the huge containers. A voice called out from somewhere in the distance. The shadows from the huge cranes swept across the ground. He knew Spanton was somewhere over to his right, behind one of the other containers. His eyes darted everywhere, his finger poised delicately on the trigger, ready to squeeze it in an instant. He came to the end of the container and a figure emerged from the parallel one. Instinctively, Noonan raised the gun, but saw at the last possible moment that it was Spanton and he instantly lowered it, his heart thudding in his chest. Then suddenly at the edge of a further container, a third figure emerged.

"Down!" shouted Noonan. Spanton dropped to the ground. The dark figure spun round, and Noonan fired once. The figure fell back against the container, crying out once. Then his body slid down and was still. Spanton got up and they raced to the body. The young man, who could be no more than twenty-five, was not quite dead, but he was clearly not long for this world either. The bullet had torn through his neck and blood was pumping arterially out onto the tarmac. Noonan had gone for a chest shot but visibility was poor, and the shot had gone wide. The young man's eyes stared up at the sky, seeing nothing. He moaned a couple of times, almost sounding like a child. Noonan turned away helplessly and instantly felt a tingle creeping down his spine. Standing several feet away, he saw – or thought he saw – Spender in the shadows, watching him. His thin, pale face loomed out at him from the darkness. Clearly, he had just witnessed everything that had happened. Spender! What the hell...? Noonan began moving towards him, as though he were an iron filament being drawn towards a magnet. Spender stepped backwards, melting back into the shadows. By the time Noonan had got to where Spender had been standing, there was no sign of him. His eyes darted anxiously all around, but Spender had seemingly vanished into thin air. And then Noonan began to feel waves of sickness. A voice suddenly sounded from somewhere close by, but Noonan barely heard it.

"Thanks," said Spanton quietly. But Noonan was already walking away, feeling the bile rising in him. He fought to keep it down, desperately resisting the temptation to vomit. He wanted no-one to see him like this. For a moment, he saw Anna in his mind. Then he cursed Lomax furiously. He thought he had left all this behind. And now there were six vicious bastards dead – and for what? To protect one more vicious bastard that the world would be a better place without.

Noonan staggered back to the strip, his face suddenly pale and ill-looking. He dropped the gun back into his pocket unconsciously. The other five were spread out in a semi-circle. They all turned to face him. The smell of cordite hung horribly in the air. Spanton was looking at him oddly.

"Are you alright?" he asked.

"What the hell do you think?" snapped back Noonan angrily. He realised then that his anger was merely a device to cover up his own sense of horror and self-disgust. Then he forced himself to relax and looked at Lomax, waiting for his instructions. Police sirens began to wail somewhere in the distance, steadily getting louder.

"Let's get out of here," Lomax said, after what seemed like an eternity.

<u>9</u>

The police sirens were sounding uncomfortably close, perhaps now only three blocks away. Noonan reflected grimly as he started to run that there must be a police station much closer to the docks than they had imagined. That was typical of his luck right now. As the old saying went, there was never a policeman around when you wanted one; the inevitable flipside to that was that when you really didn't want one, there was no getting away from them. The thought nagged away at him as he made his way back to the car, throwing himself into the driver's seat and firing up the engine. He heard the other doors slamming before he reversed the car and drove around the boxes, tearing through the gears as he did so. The Mercedes swerved out of the warehouse and onto the approach road. As Noonan turned right at the end of the road, the first of the police cars swept past them with its screaming, sickening siren and blazing blue light.

"Easy, Noonan," said Lomax as Noonan instinctively slowed the car to an unhurried cruise. He found himself grinding his teeth together in effort not to snarl back at Lomax. A fleet of white police cars rocketed past them then, lights flashing, but none of them tried to stop them. Noonan turned to look at Katharina sitting next to him in the passenger seat. Despite the cold, her forehead was glistening with sweat, and her face was ghostly white. She was shaking slightly. He glanced in the rear-view mirror. Lomax was seated to the right, as earlier, Brewster on the left, with Spanton sandwiched between them. Spanton's eyes were darting excitedly, his facial muscles twitching. Lomax's gun was still in his hand, louchely covering all of them. His face however typically betrayed no emotion. Opposite him Brewster was clutching a suitcase to his chest. He was staring at a point through the front windscreen into the dark night. He seemed in a zone entirely of his own, as if the car and the rest of them in it simply didn't exist. Noonan concentrated on the road again. He saw a sign up ahead for the A1089, which he gratefully took. It wasn't until he was safely on it that he started to relax.

"Take the A13 when it comes up," Lomax instructed Noonan, "and turn that radio on." Noonan did not reply, simply glanced at him in the mirror. He then leaned forward and turned the knob. The crackle of the radio filled the car. As Noonan had guessed, Lomax's radio was tuned into a police radio frequency. That dial had probably been fixed and not moved since Lomax had bought the car. Noonan had somehow never seen Lomax as a Radio 2 man. The harsh, barely discernible voices from the police radio faded in and out. From what could be pieced together, men were being drafted into the area and it was being combed, but so far, no descriptions had been circulated.

"Ok, we're clear," Lomax murmured, with no sense of relief. "Turn the radio off". Noonan shot him a doubtful look. "Do it," Lomax confirmed. Noonan reached down and snapped the radio off. Fifteen minutes later, the sign pointing to the junction leading to the A13 shone brightly in the car headlights. Noonan

110

indicated and moved smoothly onto the A13.

The A13 took them quickly into South Essex. At the Stanford-le-hope bypass, Lomax suddenly instructed, "Come off here!" Noonan had been wondering for a while exactly where Lomax was taking them, but he did as he was instructed. It would do no good to ask and he would find out soon enough anyway. They passed through several villages, then the main road narrowed into a dark, country lane. The flat, featureless Essex countryside stretched out all around them, swamped in blackness. For several minutes there was no sign of civilisation or light anywhere. An occasional car hissed past. They approached a turning to the left at the edge of a field and Lomax told Noonan to take it. This road was, if anything, even darker and narrower than the one before and Noonan began to worry that Lomax was driving them out to the middle of a field to swiftly execute them. Out in this black, bleak emptiness it might be days before their bodies were discovered. But straight away Noonan dismissed this as illogical; Lomax had gone to a lot of trouble to get them all together and there would be a good reason for that. The blackness was now so complete that he was unable to see any of the others in the car. The headlights cut through the dark haze into nothing. With Lomax in the back seat and nothing outside the window, this was starting to feel like a journey into Hell. Eventually however Noonan was able to pick out a church turret in the distance and a sign announcing the village of Tepping. They rode through it and five minutes later, a track led off to the right.

"Down there," ordered Lomax. Noonan turned down a dark, muddy track leading to a low, white, remote farm building, with a wide barn to the right. A decrepit looking old tractor could be glimpsed parked just inside it. Noonan parked next to the thick, oaken front door.

"Right, out you get," was Lomax's final instruction. He handed Noonan a key ring with two keys. Noonan opened the front door with the first one he tried. He walked into a dark, cold corridor. He turned a light on. The others followed him in with Lomax bringing up the rear, his gun still in his hand. There was a door at the end leading into a large drawing room, which had been emptied of furniture so

that just a wooden table with four chairs
and a large projection screen against the
far wall were visible. A projector was set
up and ready to go on the opposite wall.
Lomax was well organised. Lomax walked
round to the far side of the table and placed
his open briefcase on it.

"Right, the guns; put them back in
the case. Brewster, I want yours too." The
four of them looked at each other, as if
trying to arrive at a decision by committee.
Finally, it was Spanton who moved first,
pulling the gun from his belt while
fastening the safety catch. He dropped the
gun into the case. Brewster also took his
Walther from his coat pocket and weighed
it in his hand. He looked back at Lomax,
his mind calmly and thoroughly assessing
the situation. Finally, he shrugged, and
stepped forward, dropping the gun into the
briefcase. Then Spanton and Brewster
froze. On the other side of the room,
Katharina had raised her gun and was now
aiming it at Lomax's head. She stood with
both feet apart, the gun firmly gripped
with both hands.

Lomax appeared once again
unperturbed. A slight smile formed at the

side of his lips. "Yes," he nodded. "I thought you'd be the one."

Katharina lifted her thumb and pulled back the hammer on the gun. The sharp, metallic click sounded surprisingly loud in the cold, stark, near-empty room. She lifted the gun a fraction higher. "I want no part of this," Katharina told Lomax shakily, her German accent thickening. "I've already killed once tonight because of you. Maybe I should kill you next." Could she kill this man? As she looked into the dark, opaque holes of his eyes and his unworried expression, she suddenly realised how hopeless her situation had become. This man was totally in control of all of them. She also became aware that Noonan had appeared to her right, standing right up close. Lomax took a couple of steps forward until the gun barrel was only a foot away from his face. He remained completely calm.

"You've got ten seconds to hand that over," he told her in a quiet, reasonable voice. His eyes looked beyond the gun and bored into hers. For a few moments the air in the room felt charged with electricity. No-one moved.

Finally, it was Noonan who spoke. "He means it, Katharina."

In the space of a heartbeat Lomax had shot forward like a cobra. His left thumb was suddenly under the hammer of the gun and his right was ripping it out of her hands. He eased the hammer gently back and dropped the gun into the briefcase. "Good girl," he said. "That wasn't so hard now, was it?" Then with lightning-fast timing and precision, his right hand flew out, the fingers flat against each other. He smacked Katharina hard across the face, the force of the blow knocking her backwards. She let out a shriek of pain and shock, her body falling back against the wall. She landed in a heap on the wooden floor, dazed. Noonan rushed over to where she had fallen. She put a hand to her face, which now throbbed with pain. For a moment she was disorientated. Noonan leaned in and helped her back to her feet, but then suddenly she was pulling away from him, angry.

"Get away from me!" she barked. Then she turned and glowered at him. "Whose side are you on anyway?"

"Yours," Noonan replied. Katharina looked away, folding her arms. Noonan glared furiously at Lomax; his eyes filled with hate.

"You did the sensible thing, Noonan", Lomax told him. "Remember what's at stake here." Noonan felt the words shoots through him like bolts of lightning. Then Lomax looked across at Spanton and Brewster. Spanton's mouth had fallen open, while Brewster's expression had not changed. Everything about Spanton, from the extravagant way he had checked his gun to the nervousness he had displayed in the car after the shooting, marked him out as a potential loose cannon. His skill, courage and training were obvious, but Spanton was going to be a worry for him. He had a different problem with Brewster, who simply remained for the moment enigmatic, unreadable.

Lomax held his hand out to Noonan, who pulled the gun out of his coat pocket and handed it over. Lomax pointed to the projector. "The projector, Noonan." Noonan held Lomax's gaze for as long as he dared; he wanted to be as obstructive as possible without endangering himself or

116

the others. Then after a few seconds he walked over and turned on the projector. Lomax had him on remote control and he was hating every second of it. But for the time being he would just have to swallow it. Lomax went to the light switch and dimmed them, picking up a control for the projector as he did so. "Sit down, all of you." His voice was cold, distant.

The four of them took seats around the table. Lomax pressed a switch, and an aerial view of an upmarket area in London flashed up in front of them.

"This is Knightsbridge," began Lomax. He picked up a small wooden ruler that was leaning up against the wall and, leaning in, pointed the end at a large square in the centre of the map. "And right here is the Central Bank."

Noonan felt his mouth go dry. So, this was it! Lomax had brought them all together to break into a vault. But for what? Cash? Diamonds? Noonan immediately felt the paranoia starting to creep beneath his skin. This felt too ordinary for Lomax. What would he want from a bank?

"And inside the vaults – six million in diamonds."

"*"Das ist verrückt...*," muttered Katharina under her breath.

"And we're going to take it out of there," continued Lomax. "The diamonds belong to a certain militant organisation in the Middle East whose political views run contrary to our own. The diamonds are in a safety deposit box and are being used to fund their operations over here, which have already included several acts of terror. By relieving them of the diamonds, we strangle their funds, and they can't operate. You've been brought in because this cannot be seen to be a legitimate operation. This must appear to be a conventional robbery. To that end you will grab as many of the other safety deposit boxes as you can. If anyone's caught in there, which you shouldn't be, this would appear to be just another failed bank robbery. No-one will help you and you will be charged accordingly. Do as I say, however, and you'll have nothing to worry about. If you pull this off successfully, you'll all be set up with new identities and allowed to disappear again. You'll get your lives back."

118

Spanton whistled to himself. Lomax leaned in again and pointed to an area right at the end of the block. "We begin here – at the art gallery. We go round the side of the building after closing time, then we get onto the roof. Spanton, you're an expert climber, so you'll help us get to the top. Then we go over the roofs..." Lomax was describing the route with the end of his ruler... "Until we get to the bank – here. Then we go down. I've studied this bank carefully. It's the only way in. The vaults are underground..." He paused. "Then when we've got what we came for we go out through a small door at the back leading into Basil Street." Lomax pointed vaguely at a point on the map.

At this point Brewster stood up and picked up the suitcase. "I've heard enough," he told Lomax. "Good luck with it, but I'm out."

Brewster started walking to the door. The familiar click of the Browning .9mm in Lomax's hand stopped him. Brewster smiled grimly to himself and turned round. Lomax was aiming the gun at his head.

"Don't be naïve, Brewster." There was a deadly tone to Lomax's voice. "Do you really think I can let you walk out of here? Bring the suitcase over."

With sullen resignation, Brewster walked slowly forward with it and held it up to Lomax by the handle.

"Put it down slowly and move back," Lomax ordered. Brewster did as he was told. "You might get it back after the job. If you do well."

Brewster looked hard at Lomax. "Look, Lomax, the job can't be done – I've tried it!"

"I know," replied Brewster, his eyes glittering fiercely, his moustache twitching with excitement. "That's why you're here!"

Brewster sat down slowly, his facial muscles tautening. "You're out of your mind, Lomax."

"Six months ago, Caldwell set up the very same job. There were four of you. You were the only one who got away. The others are all serving life sentences. It's just as well they kept your name out of it, isn't it?"

Brewster remained silent.

"Well, you're about to have another crack at it, Brewster.   And this time it's going to work.   You're going to get inside that vault.   You know all about the alarm systems inside that place.   And you know exactly how to get past them.   You worked very hard on it."

"How would you know?"

"I know everything I need to know about you, Brewster."

"Then you'll know there's an alarm that runs straight through to the police station only fifteen minutes away."

"Yes; that's what tripped you up the last time, wasn't it?   You tunnelled in from the office complex next door.   That was where you went wrong."   Lomax then looked over at Katharina. "Miss Vogel will get us first into the vault and then into the safety deposit box.   She's an expert with explosives.   I recognised her handiwork from that bank in Germany.   And I want her to do the same thing here."

Katharina looked anxiously at the other three, but they were all looking directly at Lomax.

"*Scheisen...*" she just muttered in a doomed whisper.

"Noonan and I will be handling all the finer stuff." Then he turned to the others. "Questions?"

"When do we go in?" Noonan asked.

Lomax took a step forward. "Four days from now," he replied.

PART II

10

Noonan lifted the axe into the air and brought it down hard into the bark of the tree with a concentrated and coordinated ferocity. A drop of sweat formed on his forehead, slid downwards, and dropped softly to the mud. His face throbbed with warmth from the effort of swinging the axe. His eyes remained fixed on the deep yellow wound in the tree as he relentlessly drove the axe into it and the tree coughed out its splinters. At times when Noonan needed all his mental powers to focus on a problem, he would engage in intense and physical work like this. He was not only concerned with the perplexing riddle of Lomax's bank job, but also with the riddle of Spender. The job sounded credible enough, but Noonan had instantly distrusted Lomax. There was more to this job than he was letting on. Of that he was certain. He also felt certain that he had seen Spender in the shadows that evening on the dock and had not imagined it. Spender was expecting a call from him. At present, however, under Lomax's watchful eyes, he could do nothing.

It had been two days since Noonan and the others had first learned of Lomax's plan and they were still stationed at Lomax's Essex farmhouse. He could however see how their present location would suit Lomax's purposes ideally. It was as remote a property as one could possibly imagine. It lay at the end of a half-mile long track and the village of Tepping, the closest evidence of nearby civilisation, was about three miles away. Following their arrival on that first evening, a surly, scowling brute was introduced to them by Lomax as Ackland, the groundsman, but it was immediately clear that his real purpose was to act as an extra pair of eyes. They were all under constant, intense scrutiny, completely cut off and isolated from everything, which is exactly what Lomax would have had in mind.

They had all eaten together in the evening. Conversation had been limited to a series of grunts and curt exchanges. Noonan did not enjoy eating with others and he had decided that he would eat alone for the rest of the time he had to stay here, no matter what Lomax insisted on. He had presumed that Ackland had prepared the minced meat and potatoes that they had been forced to eat. If so, his skills in the kitchen were about as appealing as the rest of him.

The farmhouse had five bedrooms, which was handy, though Noonan's room was barely large enough for a single bed. No doubt Lomax had personally selected this room just for him, out of spite. The other bedrooms, from what he had seen, were all much bigger, but Noonan had much greater problems to worry about. In fact, the room turned out to be another poignant and heart-breaking reminder of Anna, for it was no bigger than the one he had shared with her at Mr Burton's farm. And the farm itself stood in stark contrast to Mr Burton's, which had been full of warmth and love; Lomax's farm by comparison was Colditz without swastikas and guard towers. There were even vertical iron bars across the windows. Only Lomax would feel at home in a place like this, assuming he did in fact own it. The property was a sickly shade of white, two storeys high, with a tiled roof a dull shade of brown. The surrounding grounds were all stretches of mud, sectioned off by wire fences. A small cluster of trees stood defiantly to the back of the house, and this was where Noonan had decided to spend his time, keeping himself as far away from the others as possible. There was a small shed behind the house, which Noonan had made a point of investigating later. Aside from the Malayan jungle, it was the most God-forsaken place he had ever seen.

Noonan had cut over halfway through the tree. He stopped for a moment, lowering the axe to the ground. Ackland was watching him a small distance away, but Noonan deliberately blotted him from his consciousness. He leaned into the handle and allowed himself to get his breath back. His face now felt on fire and the hair on his temple felt damp. He looked at the dry leaves on the ground. There was no telephone in the farmhouse. As they had driven through Tepping, Noonan had noticed a red telephone box on the green.   That was about three miles away.   Nonetheless, he had to get to it and use it to call Spender. But how he could get there and back undetected would be a serious problem. Every time he had looked up, he had seen Lomax or Ackland close by on some part of the estate, watching everything.   Ackland had black hair and even blacker eyes.   He had not spoken a word since the previous day, merely hovered menacingly in the background.   Even when he wasn't in the room, Noonan could feel his presence in every part of the house.   Noonan imagined snapping his neck and would enjoy every moment of it.   Noonan lifted the axe again and started back on the tree.   It was Monday now.   The job was scheduled for Thursday.

As much as he tried to focus entirely on his present situation, the spectre of Anna kept looming over him. He kept thinking of the curt goodbye note that he had been forced to write to her before walking out of her life on Christmas Eve.   He knew that it would have broken her heart as it had broken his.   Until the day he saw her again, he knew that the pain of that final note would never stop

129

tearing into him. It had been the cruellest, most destructive act he had ever committed against another human being, and it had been against the only woman he had ever loved. Could she ever forgive him? Would she have really believed that he would just leave like that? And soon after, Lomax had snatched her and was holding her somewhere. He could barely think about it.

So many questions crashing through his beating skull and no possible answers. And just where on Earth was Lomax holding her? Would Spender be able to find her? The axe smashed relentlessly away at the hole in the tree, faster, faster, *faster...* The sweat was now cascading down his forehead and into his eyes, causing them to sting fiercely. Then he heard the groan. He stepped back and looked up. The tree was swaying and began to topple away from him. It crashed to the ground with a loud thud. Lomax had sent him out in the morning to gather firewood and he was glad to have had a task to be getting on with to help pass the time.

As he started in on the fallen trunk, he felt a movement behind him. Spanton was standing behind him, watching him with an amused look in his eye. Noonan blinked, clearing his eyes of the sweat. How long he had been standing there? Noonan dropped the axe and stared back at him.

Spanton smiled briefly and walked forward. Noonan picked up the axe. Spanton sat down on the bark where Noonan was about to strike. Noonan dropped the axe again. Spanton was fixing him with a challenging smile. "Don't say much, do you?" was all he said.

"What's there to say?" Noonan replied.

"Not much, I guess," replied Spanton. "You were in the army, weren't you?"

"That's right." Noonan took a couple of steps to his right and started hacking away at the fallen trunk.

"I was in the Royal Marines. They still want thirty years of my life."

"So, I hear."

"My Master-At-Arms tried pushing his luck with me. So, I broke his back and then his neck."

"Yeah, I heard that too." Noonan's axe continued to crash down. Spanton crossed his leg over his knee and sat relaxed. Noonan's annoyance at his presence was obvious and Spanton was clearly relishing every moment of it.

"Well, that's what happens when people think they can push me. I just want to be sure of you if we're going to work together, Noonan."

"Don't worry, I want to keep both my back and my neck. Besides, what chance would I have against a disgraced ex-Marine?"

Spanton laughed then. "You know, I might end up quite liking you, Noonan." Noonan squinted at him enquiringly, then got back to work. "What makes you so special, Noonan? Why did Lomax go out of his way to select you?"

"Ask him."

For a few moments, Spanton just sat and watched Noonan working on the trunk.   Then finally he asked, "How good are you, Noonan?"

"Good enough," was the swift reply,

Spanton watched Noonan for another few moments, then suddenly he grabbed the axe and stood up.   Noonan looked into Spanton's eyes, which were now flashing with feverish excitement. Spanton managed to wrench the axe away and toss it into the grass.   Spanton took a few steps back, then threw his fists out, assuming the combat position.   Over Spanton's shoulder, Noonan could see Ackland looking around for Lomax, unsure what to do.   Then he started to run forward, stopping a safe distance away. "Come on then, Noonan.   Show me how good you really are," grinned Spanton.

Noonan braced himself as Spanton came at him.   Noonan managed to block the first blow, then the second.   But then Spanton pulled back and brought his foot up, which caught Noonan on the chin. Noonan staggered back, suddenly dazed, and immediately angry.   He could feel it surging through his veins.   Spanton came at him again and this time Noonan was ready for him.   He ducked to the side and

133

came back with a blow to the side of Spanton's head. Spanton fell backwards but managed to straighten himself. When he looked back at Noonan, his eyes were blazing with madness and fury. Noonan could see that if Spanton carried on like this he would quickly lose control of himself, which was the last thing he needed. Spanton yelled out and came for Noonan. Both bodies locked together, and they were quickly trading and blocking blows. Noonan was becoming angrier and Spanton was becoming crazier. Noonan picked up Spanton's body and charged towards the nearest tree with it, smashing Spanton's body up against the trunk. Spanton was momentarily winded, then managed to grab a branch with both hands. He lifted his legs into the air and kicked back at Noonan, who stumbled backwards. Spanton rushed at him again, but Noonan was ready for him, and he aimed a blow at his chin, which connected and sent him spinning to the ground. His eyes still blazing furiously, Spanton sprung up from the ground and straight into Lomax, who had appeared suddenly from out of nowhere. Lomax chopped downwards viciously, cutting Spanton to the ground and keeping him there.

Spanton lay dazed for several seconds, moaning, before his body stirred. He lay on his side and raised himself onto his right elbow. Lomax walked over to where Noonan's axe lay on the ground and picked it up. Spanton painfully got to his feet, rubbing the side of his stomach. Lomax was suddenly in front of him, right up close. He thrust the axe into Spanton's hand.

"Try that," Lomax sneered nastily to him, indicating over to where Noonan stood a few feet away, breathing heavily. "Now see if you can take him!"

Noonan immediately turned his attention back to Spanton. Spanton, his eyes flashing wildly, stepped carefully towards him, the axe raised in both hands. Noonan warily kept his eyes fixed on the blade. He brought his hands up, ready to grab the handle as soon as it came flying down towards him.

Spanton suddenly let out a primal, animal-like roar. He twisted his body and forcefully plunged the axe into the bark lying on the ground. The blade penetrated deeply into the wood, the handle momentarily shaking with the force of the blow.   Noonan took a step back and slowly lowered his arms.   Spanton turned to him one last time.   His face now looked resigned, worn out.

"You're good," he told Noonan in a quiet, exhausted voice.   Then he turned and looked over to where Lomax was standing a few feet away, shaking his head in mock pity.   Spanton shot him a look of pure venom before turning and walking away, his body moving slowly through the woods.

Noonan now felt the anger surging up through him.   His face was on fire, his hair dampened with sweat, which poured into his eyes, stinging them.   He blinked to clear his vision.   Lomax was standing in front of him, gloating.   No longer feeling in control of his actions, he ripped the axe from the bark and started in towards Lomax.   Lomax just smiled horribly at him.   Noonan lunged viciously at him, swinging the axe in the air, and bringing the blade down on Lomax.   But Lomax smoothly, effortlessly, had raised his arms and taken hold of the handle, halting the arc of the axe in mid-air.   For a moment Noonan tried to wrestle the axe out of Lomax's fierce grip but was unable to.   He

simply had no strength left in him.   He
looked up into Lomax's calm, amused eyes.

"You'll never do it, Noonan," he told
him quietly.   "You want to see your girl
again, don't you?"   Noonan looked
furiously into Lomax's eyes for a few
seconds.   Then he pushed away from
Lomax and turned away.   His time would
come.   Noonan closed his eyes for a second,
then turned around.   Lomax was gone.
The axe was propped up against a tree,
waiting for him.   He walked over to it and
picked it up.   His head throbbed slightly,
but not too badly.   Now he was convinced:
Spanton was a bomb who just needed a
fuse.   He would have to watch him very
carefully from now on.   Noonan looked
once in the other direction and froze.
Leaning against a tree, having witnessed
the whole spectacle, was Brewster.   He
was still dressed elegantly in his suit and
was smoking a cigarette.   He watched
Noonan with a cool, analytical expression.
After a few seconds, he flicked the cigarette
away, ground it into the dirt with his black,
polished shoe, and turned and walked
away.   Noonan watched him go.   Then he
lifted the axe and the chopping started
again.

11

Noonan stayed out till seven-thirty, by which time it was dark. It was also very cold, but he felt a warm glow at the thought of Ackland standing only a few feet away being forced to endure the cold too. He could feel the bastard's eyes burning into him through the darkness. He would gladly have ripped into him with the axe right there. Lomax had handed it to him that morning, but Noonan decided that he was going to store it in the shed; it would provide him with the perfect opportunity to see if there was anything useful in there. As he walked towards the shed, he turned and could make out Ackland's bulky figure following him every step of the way.

He pulled back the lock and stepped into the shed. As he had predicted, it was full of tools that looked like they had been hanging around for a good fifty years. Noonan could see nothing that would immediately benefit him. As he had expected, the door opened a few seconds later, and Ackland stood there, glowering disdainfully at him. Noonan looked around the walls, found a pair of nails and used them to hang the axe. Then he turned and walked out without even a glance at Ackland.

He went back to the wheelbarrow into which he had gathered a pile of thick, heavy logs and pushed it back towards the house. He was unloading the logs onto the porch when Ackland walked past him, leaving the front door open. Noonan gave the wheelbarrow a furious kick, sending it spinning clumsily onto the gravel, and walked angrily into the house.

The kitchen was on the right and his stomach was now growling furiously for food. He opened the door, hoping to find the kitchen empty. Only Katharina was in there, standing at the oven, stirring something in a large saucepan. A cigarette burned in an ashtray next to her. She was wearing her khaki sweater and dark jeans. She looked to Noonan so much like the German terrorist she obviously was that she may as well have been attending an open casting call. What a bunch he had landed up with: a gangster, a terrorist, and a psychopath. So, what was his role in all this? Perhaps he was a little of all three. But one thing he was sure of: for as long as Lomax was around, and Noonan was against him, then he had to be on the right side, however he was to be pigeonholed. Katharina stopped stirring, picked up the cigarette, took a long pull on it, and turned to face Noonan.

"What's for supper?" he asked.

"Why don't you make it and find out?" she replied in a brittle tone.

Noonan walked in and closed the door behind him. He walked up to the saucepan and saw scrambled eggs bubbling inside. After several hours of hard labour, the smell of the eggs was delicious, and Noonan felt his stomach throbbing in anticipation. He waited for her to pour the eggs onto a plate and sit down at the nearby wooden table. He was quietly annoyed. He needed privacy and did not want to eat in the company of a female terrorist. He was too hungry and tired however to wait any longer. There were four eggs left in an open box, a loaf of sliced bread and a bottle of milk on the sideboard. He began to prepare a plate of scrambled eggs as the girl had done. He deliberately avoided eye contact with the girl but could sense her occasionally looking over in his direction. He could hear her cutlery delicately scraping away against the plate and tried to block her out. He dragged out the process of making the eggs in the hope that she would finish and leave, but she stubbornly remained where she was. He silently cursed her.

Five minutes later, his scrambled eggs on toast ready, he moved to the table, choosing the seat directly opposite her. She had nearly finished her meal by the time he was beginning his. It was the girl who finally broke the silence.

"You don't like me, do you?" she asked in an emotionless voice, which implied that she cared nothing for whatever the answer might be. It was not an answer that required much thinking on his part.

"What's there to like?" he simply replied.

"Well, that's not important right now," she continued in her hard German voice. "Because I might just be your best chance of staying alive. And you might be mine." The tip of her cigarette glowed fiercely, and she exhaled, blowing the smoke over Noonan's head. "I know what you must think of me: a killer, a fanatic..."

"I don't just think it," Noonan replied. "I've seen what you people do. So, spare me your justification."

"You people can only think in terms of statistics, crime sheets," she retorted. "You never see the provocation."

Noonan lustily shovelled the eggs into his mouth, the hot taste warming his entire body, and refused to elaborate. He felt strength immediately returning to him.

"Look, Noonan, we both know that Lomax is going to turn us in once he's got whatever he wants out of that bank," Katharina continued. "Maybe even kill us. So, if we're going to stay alive, we must trust each other, whether we like it or not."

Noonan continued to eat. He had distrusted Katharina from the moment he

142

had met her and had no intention of starting now. In fact, he had no more reason to trust her than he did Lomax. She would kill him in an instant if she needed to.

"What has Lomax got on you?" she then asked. "You already know about me."

Noonan had to concede that she had a point. Yet he was still not prepared to divulge any personal information to a woman he so actively disliked.

"OK, so you won't tell me," Katharina continued. "Have it your way. But you'll have to trust me sooner or later. You don't believe that this is about diamonds at all, do you?" There was a pause before she continued. "You used to work for Lomax. What happened?" She waited for a reply. "Are you going to tell me?"

"No."
"You're a fool, Noonan," she replied. "I can't help you if you won't help me."

"What did you have in mind?"

Katharina lowered her voice and leaned forward a little.

"As soon as this job is over, we kill Lomax - before he has a chance to kill us."

"And what about the other two?"

She shrugged. "Why trust them?"

"Why trust me?" He took another mouthful of eggs. "Lomax was right about you. You really are ruthless, aren't you?"

"Just practical. I'll do whatever I have to do to survive." Noonan looked up into her dark, sombre eyes for the first time since he had entered the room. They were staring defiantly back at him. He searched her face for some sense of vulnerability, some betrayal of a hidden emotion that he was not supposed to see, but he could detect none. Her eyes hardened. "Don't you see, we have no choice?"

Noonan suddenly felt Anna's spirit in the room. He felt her warmth and her love in stark contrast to Katharina's coldness, viciousness, and duplicity. And he suddenly felt anger burning in the pit of his stomach. He stared hard into her eyes.

"Now listen. For reasons I don't have to explain to you I need Lomax alive.

So, if you try and kill him, I'll kill you myself. Do you understand?"

"You'll never have that chance, Noonan."

At that moment, the door opened, and Ackland came in. Noonan felt his body stiffen. Ackland positioned himself by the door and watched them, disinterested. Noonan diffused his anger by focussing on Katharina's deep brown eyes. They stared back at him almost without expression. Noonan wolfed down his meal quickly, but the pleasure of it was compromised by Ackland's glare, which Noonan could always sense in the corner of his eye. Finally, he could take no more. He finished his final mouthful, slammed his knife and fork down, and whipped his head round to face Ackland.

"Do you mind not staring?" he barked furiously. Ackland's eyes burned with unrestrained meanness. That was enough for Noonan. He pushed his chair back, strode furiously over, and stood facing him. Ackland's eyes burned with a venomous fire. Noonan could feel the anger throbbing right through to his fists.

Then suddenly he became aware of a breeze cutting across his face. He turned. Lomax had just entered the room and was standing in the doorway, looking from one to the other. His eyes settled on Ackland.

"That's enough, Ackland. Go and see to Brewster, will you?"

Ackland held Noonan's gaze for a few more seconds before he reluctantly moved away and left the room. Lomax watched him leave, then just stood in the doorway watching them. He had a cold smile on his face, as if he knew every word of the conversation they had just had and knew exactly what their intentions were. And then, just as suddenly, the door closed, and he was gone again. Noonan and Katharina looked at each other, each trying to read the other's thoughts. It suddenly felt very cold in that kitchen.

Ten minutes later, Noonan moved noiselessly through the hallway by the front door. The sound of a television set blasted through the open living room door. Noonan stood in the doorway looking at the television flickering away in the corner of the room.   An armchair had been pulled up in front of the screen, though the occupant could not be seen.   The face of the middle-aged,   greying,   bespectacled newsreader filled the screen as he unsmilingly delivered the latest headlines: *"... The mysterious disappearance of West African state leader Dr Julius Obana is still being investigated by Scotland Yard. Dr Obana was in this country seeking military support for his state as it descends further into civil war..."*   The words washed over Noonan.   Current events happening in the outside world he could barely relate to right now.   *"...Police are yet to identity the body found on the Central line two days ago, though they have confirmed that the victim was male, in his early forties, and possibly foreign..."* Already it felt like a lifetime ago to Noonan.   Just then, the body shifted in the armchair, and Lomax's eyes were suddenly peering over the back of the chair right at him, devouring him.   Noonan had not made a sound and yet Lomax had known he was there.

"Sound familiar, Noonan?"   His tone was harsh, accusatory.   He then dropped back into the armchair and paid

Noonan no further mind. Noonan turned
and noiselessly walked away again.

He climbed the stairs. On the
landing he turned to see Ackland standing
on the stairs looking up at him. Noonan
moved carefully along the corridor.
Spanton's door was open. Noonan looked
in and saw him kneeling, both hands
outstretched, both loaded down with a pile
of heavy books. Spanton was grimacing
and groaning with the pain, his eyes
screwed shut, and his legs wobbling
furiously with the effort. Sweat was
breaking out on his forehead. His eyes
suddenly snapped open, and he looked
directly at Noonan, his eyes sparkling with
concentration, pain, and loathing.

Noonan walked past the bathroom.
Leaning in the doorway was Brewster,
with the same enigmatic look on his face.
He beckoned Noonan into the bathroom
with a casual flick of the head. Noonan
followed him inside, intrigued. Brewster
closed the door softly.

"I've got to tell you something."
Brewster said calmly, pointed towards the
door in the direction of Spanton's room.
"That guy's crazy. I mean really nuts."

"That's what you want to tell me?" Noonan replied. "I'd already worked that out for myself." Noonan wondered what was coming next. The evening was taking another very strange turn.

"Alright, Noonan. I want to know what the hell's going on around here." Brewster spoke evenly but with an edge. "One minute I'm getting out of the country and the next I'm being forced into some robbery by some lunatic who claims to be working for the government."

Noonan shrugged. "Same for the rest of us."

Brewster's eyes narrowed. "I want answers, Noonan. Who the hell is Lomax and what does he want with me?"

"Lomax works for the government. That much is true." Noonan looked into Brewster's eyes, wondering if he could trust him. His blue-grey eyes were clear and seemed incapable of hiding anything.

"Is this operation really on the level?"

Noonan shrugged. "I know only what you know."

"He's not going to let any of us disappear after the job, is he?"

"That's the one thing you can be sure about."

Brewster's eyes glittered fiercely and then he smiled for a second before his face became a rigid mask again. "Look, Noonan, this bank; it can't be done. I've tried it. It can only go one of two ways: we either spend the rest of our lives in prison or we all end up dead." Noonan remained silent, waiting for Brewster to continue. "Six months ago, my firm tried to take that bank. I studied all the alarm systems, knew them backwards. We should have been out of there and away. But the police were waiting for us."

"That's what Lomax said. You were the only one who got away."

"Right, and I'm not going back into that place again. I'm telling you, there are systems in there that not even the top brass at the bank knows about."

"Lomax would know about them. He doesn't move until he knows absolutely everything there is to know."

"Well, he's nuts if he thinks he can pull this off. He's more than welcome to try it, so are you, but you can count me out."

"So, what are you going to do?"

"I'm getting out of here, what do you think?"

"You won't make it, Brewster."

Brewster's eyes became fierce and combative.

"Why not?"

"Because that's what Lomax thinks you're going to do. Believe me, he's got us all worked out. He'll figure you're going to try and run. And he'll be waiting for you."

Brewster studied him for a moment. "You're really scared of him, aren't you?"

"If you had any sense, you'd be too."

"Well, maybe Lomax should be scared of me."

Noonan shook his head. "You don't know Lomax. Looks like you're about to get to know him better."

"Why don't you come with me, then? Two of us would stand a much better chance. You're the only one I trust. Spanton's a psychopath and I wouldn't trust that German bitch as far as I could throw her." Brewster waited for an answer, but Noonan said nothing. "Come on, what have we got to lose?"

Noonan just shook his head again. "There is a way to get him but not like this."

"So, what's your plan?"

"Right now, I haven't got one, because right now, he's got us exactly where he wants us. But at some point, there will be a moment – just one moment - when he's vulnerable; a moment when he makes a mistake. That's the time to take him. We'll just have to wait for that."

"You're not coming then?"

Noonan moved to the door and turned one last time. "You're wasting your time," he said finally before letting himself out and moving purposefully back to his room. Lomax and Ackland were nowhere to be seen. As he moved across the corridor, he noted an attic door in the ceiling, which could provide a possible

152

means of escape. He got into his room, closed the door, and lay down on the bed. He closed his eyes and went over the events of the evening. So far, of the other three, only Katharina seemed to have the measure of Lomax. She was certainly smarter than the other two. Yet forming an alliance with her was unthinkable. Brewster, on the other hand, had been right about Spanton and Katharina but had sorely underestimated Lomax. If he did try to break out, he would be handing himself to Lomax on a plate. Despite this, it was becoming clear that of the three it was Brewster he would put his trust in. He had looked into his eyes and seen the capacity for terrible violence there, but also sincerity. And what of himself? He wanted, *needed,* to get away from here too. But how could he succeed where Brewster was bound to fail? Brewster was no tougher than he was, but he was also far too sure of himself. Noonan made up his mind that he would go out the following night through the attic. For the remainder of the day, he would be watching Lomax more than Lomax would be watching him.

153

He sat up, removing his shoes, sweater, and trousers, taking his wallet out as he did so. The light from the naked bulb up above cast out a dim, yellowish hue. It was not enough light to read by, but he could still see well enough. As he had done every night for the last four months, he took out Anna's photograph and lay back on the bed. He gazed again at the girl with the wistful smile. Here he was in a cell of Lomax's making, unable to get to her and with no idea where she was. The thought fiercely dampened his spirits. Was she even this minute locked away in a tiny room much like this one? Already he felt more determined than ever to get through the following evening and all the dangerous events that would follow. Whatever happened, her spirit would be with him for every part of this treacherous journey, looking out for him and keeping him safe. He kissed her image once, put the photograph back in the wallet, reached up and turned out the light.

<u>12</u>

Noonan awoke to a terrible scream.

At first it seemed to have come from the darkest depths of his nightmares. He had struggled to let sleep wash over him as his restless mind had gone over his plan for the following day. Then finally, at around half past one, he had sunk into a shallow sleep. The scream had pierced through his dark, subconscious torment. Then he realised that his eyes were in fact wide open, and he was staring up at the black ceiling.

The scream came again. This time, Noonan rolled out of bed and pressed his face up against the bars of the window, looking out into the black night. Noonan felt his spirits plummeting as his eyes pierced the gloominess outside. He knew what he was about to see even before he saw it: three figures emerging from the darkness. The figure in the middle was crumpled and bent, the two figures on either side half-carrying, half dragging him. Lomax and Ackland's figures were immediately recognisable, tall, and invulnerable against the blackness of the night. The figure in the middle remained covered by the shadows so that he was not immediately identifiable. It was only when he lifted his head and looked up at the house, seemingly straight up at Noonan's window and into his eyes, that he could finally see Brewster's face, which was bloody, swollen and beaten, particularly around the chin.

Noonan raced to the door, flung it open and turned on the light in the landing. He crashed down the stairs, three at a time. He was dimly aware of doors opening behind him. Lomax and Ackland were already through the front door. Lomax looked up to see Noonan staring hard at him. In response, Lomax flung Brewster's limp body to the wooden floor.

"Don't touch him!" Lomax ordered. Noonan stared hard into Lomax's eyes, the fear and the hatred of the man throbbing up through his insides. Behind him he sensed Katharina and Spanton standing on either side of him, slightly back. Lomax looked at all three of them. "Brewster made a mistake tonight," he said in a cold, controlled voice. "He tried to run out on me. Noonan, pick him up and take him to the cellar. It's through that door at the end. Spanton, you help him."

Noonan lifted his finger and pointed it at Lomax. "You lay another finger..."

"Just do it or you'll be staying down there with him!" Noonan, seeing no alternative, let his anger slowly subside and took Brewster's arm, lifting him up. He examined Brewster's face: Lomax had been meticulous and careful about where he had beaten him; the eyes and the fingers were perfectly intact; Brewster would be needing them in good working order for the job ahead. "He'll mend in time for the job," Lomax continued. "I made sure of that. Otherwise, you'd be burying him."

Spanton, his face a manic mask, took the other side. Brewster lifted his head and gave Noonan a momentary glance before his head dropped again. Noonan had tried to read something into the glance but had been unable to. Suddenly he felt a blow on his right shoulder, and he pitched forward. He turned furiously and found himself staring into Ackland's disdainful eyes. Instantly he controlled himself, comforting himself with the fact that Ackland's time was fast approaching. Ackland reached to his belt and pulled out a Browning Hi-Power pistol, waving it forcefully in Noonan's direction.

"Through that door," Lomax instructed them. Noonan felt Brewster's limp body fold in against him as they dragged him across the floor. The door opened outwards. A flight of stairs led down into darkness. They took Brewster's body through the door. Above them a light came on. Lomax had obviously pressed a switch. The stairs twisted to the right and ended in another door. Noonan opened this and found himself in a small, stony, empty space, no more than six feet by eight. A single bare lightbulb hung from the ceiling. "Drop him," he heard Lomax order him. They did so, hearing Brewster's body unravel to the floor with a soft thump and a groan. A loud explosion suddenly crashed through Noonan's ears and the cellar was suddenly plunged into darkness. Noonan turned to see the automatic smoking in Ackland's hand, the pieces of the lightbulb scattered around the stony ground and Noonan's ears ringing from the harsh, unexpected crash. "Right, out, both of you," was Lomax's final instruction. Lomax and Ackland climbed back up the stairs and were waiting for them at the top, Ackland's gun covering them carefully. Lomax went back down again, and Noonan heard the door locking. He looked over at Katharina, who was giving him the look that passes between two soldiers before going forth into the crossfire. Unexpectedly, he found her look reassuring.

"Now, get some sleep, all of you," Lomax ordered, gazing at them all fiercely. Noonan walked up the stairs to his bedroom, weary and sickened. He lay down on the bed. The struggle to let sleep wash over him was about to start all over again.

Noonan's plan for the following day was to shadow Lomax wherever he went. It was time to start turning the tables. The hunter was about to become the hunted, and not a moment too soon. He only meant to stalk Lomax – the kill would come later once Anna had been returned to him. To start with, Noonan's task was made easier by the fact that Lomax did not leave the house for the first part of the day. By the early afternoon, Noonan's nerves were shrieking for Lomax to make a move. Noonan had positioned himself near the house with his axe so that he could keep an eye on it. He was desperately willing for something to happen. The palm of his hand was starting to sustain heavy blisters from the swinging of the axe. Then at half past three, something eventually did happen.

Lomax and Ackland appeared at the front door. Noonan could momentarily feel their eyes upon him as he busied himself with the logs. He waited five seconds before looking up. Lomax was giving instructions to Ackland, who was nodding in response. Then Lomax turned and started walking briskly across the lawn and onto the grounds. Ackland stepped back into the house.   Noonan looked across for Lomax's departing figure, which was striding out rapidly towards the woodland.   He waited for Lomax to make it into the trees before carefully lowering the axe and moving swiftly after him.   He made it to the woods and looked for Lomax's shadow, which had suddenly vanished.   Noonan smiled grimly to himself.   This was standard for Lomax, and he should have expected it.   So, Noonan would just have to beat him at his own game.   Noonan pressed himself against a tree and stood still, barely breathing, his ears questing urgently for any sound.   The afternoon breeze whistled through the trees but there was no sound of movement.

Noonan waited for what seemed like five minutes before hearing careful movement several feet ahead of him. Lomax was audibly on the move again but still Noonan could not see him.   Silently, steadily, Noonan edged forward, following Lomax's trail, careful to make no sound himself at all.   He moved in a semi-crouch, keeping to the cover of the trees, always watching where he was putting his feet. The woods started to slope downwards.

Lomax's figure suddenly appeared in front of him about twenty feet ahead. Noonan's heart stopped for a second and he caught his breath. Lomax was standing still, looking behind him. Noonan froze, his figure blending into the foliage around him. Then Lomax started walking again and Noonan resumed his role as his long shadow. Now at least Noonan was able to see him.

A stile appeared in a wooden fence at the bottom of the slope. Lomax stepped over this and melted into the trees beyond. Noonan stalked soundlessly after him, silently climbing the stile and gently lowering himself to the other side. He crouched, listening. Lomax was still moving, not seemingly aware of the tail. Noonan eased himself gently forward.

The woods began to open to reveal a long path with muddy tyre tracks. Long grass stretched up on either side, providing Noonan with enough cover to pursue Lomax undetected, though he had to double over to prevent the top half of his body from becoming visible. He continued along this track for five minutes, his back screaming for relief. The ground began to slope again, and the grass became thinner

162

on the ground. Noonan lowered himself to his stomach, peering through a gap in the grass. At the bottom of the slope was a barn building with the snout of a Land Rover just visibly protruding. He felt his heart thumping in his chest with excitement as he watched Lomax walking down towards the barn. He had abandoned all caution now. All Noonan had to do was watch and wait.

Lomax's figure disappeared into the shadows of the barn. A few seconds later came the sound of the Land Rover being started up. The vehicle, with Lomax at the wheel, roared out of the barn, turning hard to the right, down another mud track that would lead to the main road. So, Lomax was quietly getting out! Noonan exhaled slowly with satisfaction. His chances of breaking out this evening undetected had improved considerably and unexpectedly. With Ackland on duty, it would still be extremely hazardous, an ordeal even, but with Lomax temporarily out of the picture, at least it was no longer impossible...

<u>13</u>

At half past eleven that evening, Noonan slipped quietly out of bed and felt around for his trousers. He quickly got dressed and stood erect in the darkness, his ears questing for the slightest noise or movement. He heard nothing; the silence and blackness were absolute. He had spotted a grey trapdoor on the roof leading from the attic, and an iron drainpipe at the corner of the house and decided that this would be his best means of escape.

Noonan took the wooden chair positioned by his window, crept to the bedroom door, listened, then carefully turned the handle. He slipped out into the darkness and counted five steps down the corridor to the point where he knew he was standing directly underneath the attic door. His eyes slowly adjusted to the darkness, and he was soon able to make out the edges of the white walls and the dark blue light of the window at the end of the corridor. He carefully placed the chair directly underneath the door. The floorboards mercifully remained silent, sharing his guilty secret. Noonan stood on the chair, reached up and gently lowered the trapdoor. He grabbed the edges and pulled himself up, twisting round so that he was sitting on the edge. He listened again, but the silence maintained its vigilant watch. His lowered his right foot, clamping it around the rim of the chair and raised it. If he dropped the chair, the game would be up. He grabbed it, pulling it carefully through the square and silently pulled the door back into position. It locked with an almost inaudible click.

Noonan felt for the matches in his back pocket, struck one and the attic suddenly revealed itself in a burst of orange light. It was virtually empty but a few feet away was the grey trapdoor. Noonan took the chair, climbed up and felt around. The door lifted upwards on a lever. He pushed it as far as he could and blew the match out. He lifted himself and wriggled his way painfully through the gap, pushing the door gently back into place.

Noonan crawled to the edge of the roof and shifted his body around a full one hundred and eighty degrees, carefully lowering his left leg into the blackness until he found an adequate foothold. A chilly wind blew across his face. His right foot felt around for a foothold, which he quickly found. From that point on he was able to shin quickly and soundlessly down the drainpipe, soon feeling the soft mud under his shoes. He turned round in the thick, black shadows, pressing his back against the bricks. The dark grounds yawned out all around him.

He half-walked, half-ran quickly but silently towards the trees and shadows at the edge of the drive. It was another bitterly cold evening, and his breath was coming out in billows of steam. He held his chest in, not daring to breathe as he ran. He got to the furthest tree and dived behind it, sinking to the ground as he did so. He cupped his hand to his mouth and gratefully exhaled. His chest was throbbing with tension and excitement. He heard a scraping sound behind him and instantly rolled over onto his stomach, peering up into the darkness. A figure emerged from around the side of the house, carrying a torch. Noonan recognised Ackland's familiar bulk as he moved towards the front door. The light from his torch bobbed carefully around, briefly lighting up his section of the woods. He rolled back behind the tree. There was the sound of the front door unlocking and then closing with a final click. Noonan waited for a full minute before carefully lifting himself off the ground and moving carefully through the darkness away from the house.

He was able to see only several feet ahead of him before the darkness swallowed the trees up, but it was good enough. After four hundred metres, and with the farmhouse now a comfortable distance behind him in the darkness, he picked up his pace into a steady jog. He measured his breathing carefully, keeping a steady rhythm going by counting in his head, *"One, two, one, two..."* He figured he had about three miles to cover, and it always helped to swallow up the miles if he could think himself into the role of a machine as he ran.

Five minutes later, Noonan reached the end of the drive. He waited, seeing and hearing nothing, before turning right. The biting cold was now starting to dig into his fingers, his lungs were starting to ache, and his ears were starting to burn. Still his breath came exploding out of him like steam belching out of an old locomotive, hampering his vision. The bleak, unlit country lane continued to twist ahead of him. He reasoned that he must have been running for two miles since he had reached the road, all the while keeping to the hedge at the side. The horizon was lit then by a dull light and the distant drone of a car sounded in the distance. Noonan fell to the ground and lay still in the long grass, feeling his chest heaving against the dampness. The light in the sky became brighter and brighter until he heard the car swoosh past him. It kept going until the sound of the engine lowered to a growl. He waited a few seconds before getting to his feet and running again. Sweat was now running down his face. He squeezed his eyes tightly shut to stop the sweat getting into them. His face was feeling warm against the chilliness of the night. Still the village of Tepping did not appear. He began to privately panic; had he missed

an all-important turning, despite having
made a careful note of the village's
position? But then he turned a corner and
the village of Tepping appeared before him
in a welcome oasis of light. He found
himself now running more frantically just
to get there. He passed under the first
streetlight and peered down the lane. Yes,
there was the telephone kiosk, lit up like a
red alien pod crash-landed in the middle of
the countryside. Noonan moved into the
shadows and leaned down, resting his
hands on his knees. Sweat was pouring
down his face and his cheeks were on fire.
He stayed in that position for several
seconds, before sharply manoeuvring
himself into the kiosk and lifting the
receiver. He quickly checked his watch:
twenty past midnight; he was well within
his schedule. He wanted to get back before
two o' clock. Any later would be pushing
his luck. He could feel his hot, gasping
breath bouncing back at him from the
receiver, which smelled of cigarettes and
alcohol. He began to dial the number that
Spender had forced him to learn by heart.
The charge would automatically be
reversed. The pips brayed harshly in his
ear. A movement outside in the night
caused his heart to momentarily stop

169

beating.   A cold wave of anxiety passed over his face.   Someone was outside the telephone kiosk! Noonan looked to his left, peering through the glass that was steaming up as it caught his heavy breath. An elderly man in a thick, light brown overcoat, wearing a hat, was sitting down on the bench just outside the kiosk.   His blurry face was looking straight back at him through the glass.   Noonan found himself looking into the calm, enquiring face of Spender. He unconsciously lowered the telephone receiver and stepped out of the kiosk.

The bench was on the opposite side of the village green from the telephone. Noonan moved towards Spender as though in a dream.   Spender watched him approach, his eyes watchful and alert. Noonan sat beside him. The light emitting from the booth continued to shine out like a beacon, lighting up the faces of the two men.   A cool breeze whipped into their faces.   Noonan squinted into the black fields beyond the wooden fence, his gaze swallowed up by the impenetrable void of the night.   Noonan's mind was suddenly full of questions.

"How did you know I'd be here?" he asked.

"I would have thought you'd have figured that out. I just followed you down here. I've been watching everything that's been going on in that farmhouse since you arrived." He paused. "What have you got for me?"

"Central bank, Knightsbridge," Noonan said carefully. "Six million in diamonds, belonging to a Middle Eastern political movement. We go in two days from now."

"And the team?"

"Katharina Vogel." Noonan waited for Spender to react. When he did not, he continued. "John Brewster. Alan Spanton."

For a moment Spender remained silent. Noonan threw him a curious glance, as though wondering if he was still there.

"Quite the rogue's gallery," he finally sighed. "Katharina Vogel. That's very interesting. She's been on the missing list for a while. We had no idea she was even in this country. I'm very curious to know how Lomax knew. It would certainly put us in a strong position with the West German police if we were to hand her back to them..."

"I just want to know about Anna," Noonan interrupted, not caring to hear about Vogel. If Spender were to hand her over to the West German police, Noonan would certainly raise no objection. He waited for a reply and once again none was forthcoming. "Well, have you found her?"

"Never mind the girl for the moment. You just go through with the job exactly as planned. Just leave Lomax to me."

"Have you found her?" Noonan pressed, feeling his heart beating faster as he waited for the reply. But Spender just looked away, inhaling deeply. "You're not getting Lomax until I see the girl, Spender. That was our agreement."

"And the agreement still stands," Spender replied in a faraway voice, still looking out into the black night.

"This isn't about diamonds, is it?" Noonan continued, desperately wanting closure to the other mystery that had been plaguing him. "What are we really playing for here?"

"You're a very perceptive man, Noonan. I could use you in my department."

"What are we playing for?" Noonan repeated, his voice hardening.

Spender spoke slowly, choosing his words carefully. "What Lomax wants from that bank is a very special box."

"What are you talking about? What box? What's inside it?" The questions came tumbling out quickly, one after the other.

Spender turned back to Noonan, and for the first time looked directly into his eyes, almost through them. "All the secrets of the world," he simply replied.

"Oh, come on, what does that mean?"

"Every dirty secret that you could possibly imagine is inside it; secrets relating to all the people who are running everything in this country. That's what you'll find in there. And if you could just see inside it, I don't think you'd sleep very well at night." He paused again, breathing out slowly. "You see, it's Lomax's own safety deposit box."

"OK, so why would he be stealing his own safety deposit box?"

"Because we've been onto him for months now. He knows it. And he knows his time is running out. He's getting ready to run, but he needs that safety deposit box, that's his insurance. Without that, he's nothing. He knows he can't walk into the bank and take it away during business hours. We're watching it round the clock. We'd pick him up the moment he stepped out of that bank, and he'd lose everything. So, what better way to get the box than to stage a robbery at night, set the four of you up, and make his own getaway? We might have been none the wiser." Spender whistled through his teeth. "Lomax," he mused, "precise and professional to the last."

"If you know the box is there, why don't you just use the power of your department to retrieve it?"

"Because I want Lomax and can only arrest him officially if he's caught coming out of that bank with the box in his hands. If he manages to escape with it, he holds all the cards again. And he'll slip away forever." Spender paused. "Besides we can't be seen to have knowledge of the box. That would put us in a rather awkward position with certain governments who we rely on to have faith in us."

Noonan felt a sickness in the pit of his stomach. So that was Lomax's game! Everything fit perfectly. It was exactly the kind of ruthless double bluff that Lomax would come up with. And inevitably, once he had the box, the rest of them would be expendable.

"What happens to us once we're inside that bank?"

"We'll be on the outside waiting. As soon as Lomax comes out, we'll pick him up, along with the rest of the gang. We'll arrange for you to go free, of course. And we'll arrange for the girl to be there too."

"And if you get hold that box, what exactly do you intend to do with it?"

"Bury it."

Noonan was suddenly feeling very uncomfortable about the deal. From whatever angle he looked at it, he was dangling on a string. There was nothing to stop Spender from throwing Noonan into prison along with the others once he had Lomax and the box. Every instinct in his body told him that Spender would betray him just as quickly as Lomax would. He would put Noonan in the same cell as the others and keep him there.

"Why should I trust you?"

"Because you have no choice. You want to see your girl again, don't you?" It could have come straight out of Lomax's mouth.

Noonan looked across the horizon. A couple of lonely blackbirds, camouflaged by the night sky, called out across the eerie silence. He shivered as an icy wind blew across his face. Behind them, a lone car lit up the green, its lights peering through the darkness like a nocturnal predator. It growled past, the sound of its engine receding into the night.

Spender then made a show of peering at his watch. "Half past one.

You'd better get back." Spender stood up and started walking away.

"Wait!" Noonan felt himself pleading with Spender. Despite his feelings about him, he had started to find Spender's presence comforting and reassuring on this cold, dark, desolate night. Spender turned round suddenly. "I'm trusting you, Spender. Just have Anna with you when we come out of that bank. Otherwise, you'll never see Lomax or the box."

Spender smiled slightly. "I know this is tough for you to deal with, Noonan, but some of us are doing this sort of work precisely because we want to help people like you." He nodded his head once. "Be careful." And with that, he turned away and walked away into the night, the blackness swallowing him up. Noonan could see the moving blur of his shadow, then nothing. His footsteps receded into nothing. He suddenly felt extremely cold and very alone.

The return journey on foot did not seem nearly so long. Noonan had suddenly felt himself drawing on extra reserves of energy that he did not know he had. He jogged back along the stark, icy road, once again keeping to the hedges on the side and diving to the ground at the sound of any approaching vehicle. Only one passed by. From there, he seemed to reach the entrance of the farm in no time at all. He felt relieved; he was more than anxious to get back to his cold bed on that God-forsaken farm, away from the dangers and treacheries of this dark, chilly night. He turned into the entrance and dived into the trees, moving silently and carefully forward, his feet moving in regular, even strides. He felt good; things were working out. If he could just get from the attic back into his bedroom unseen, then it would have been a good night's work.

He bobbed and weaved skilfully through the trees. Suddenly the sky was as bright as daylight. It dazzled him and without thinking, he dropped to the ground and lay still, not daring to breathe. What the hell! He dared not move a muscle, allowing his body to sink into the ground and become part of the landscape. His ears pricked up for any sound. His spirits plummeted as he heard soft footsteps carefully approaching, the crunch on the ground getting steadily louder. A black, blurry silhouette stepped out of the darkness, the footsteps crunching crisply on the gravel.

"Stand up slowly," the eastern European voice ordered him. There was no option. Noonan got slowly to his feet, raising his hands slightly. He looked up at the sky and saw something he should have spotted in the daylight but never did: a series of small floodlights hooked up to the trees, perhaps a dozen of them in total. Their presence in daylight had been masked by the branches hanging over them. Noonan bit down hard and cursed himself for his stupid oversight. Once his eyes had adjusted to the white-hot intensity of the lights, Noonan was able to recognise the hateful face of Ackland leering at him a few feet away. His body was still, poised, ready for action. Clasped in his fist was a heavy automatic with a silencer fitted. Noonan could discern the ghastly sparkle of victory in his eyes. But if Noonan tried to disarm him from this distance, he would be dead a second later.

It was checkmate.

There was nothing Noonan could do.

"Right, step towards me, slowly," Ackland ordered him in a gravelly voice.

14

Noonan let his body relax and his arms hang at his side. The shadows to the left and right were too far away for him to make a break for; Ackland would cut him down before he had even got halfway. Rushing him was tantamount to suicide. There was only one option available to him: to entice Ackland over to him. If he stayed rooted to the spot, Ackland might eventually grow impatient and move towards him. Then when he was close enough, Noonan might be able to take him. Ackland would not have been trained to the same level as Noonan and may be susceptible to some of the more obvious tricks. Noonan knew all of them. Lomax had taught them to him, and Lomax was still the best. Noonan allowed his vision to blur slightly, and let his mind go numb.

Would Ackland fall for it? There was only one way to find out.

"I'm going to give you five seconds," Ackland growled. The hint of Eastern Europe in his voice was coming out stronger. Presumably Lomax had recruited him from the Eastern bloc. It explained his dark, pointed, Slavic features. It was the first time Noonan had heard him speak. As a bluff, it was obvious and desperate. He heard the gun click. Five seconds passed. Ackland suddenly fired, the suppressed gun giving out a sharp pop, and Noonan felt the bullet sing about three inches from his left ear. His knees buckled slightly but he immediately corrected himself. He meant to show Ackland that there was no way for him to win.

"The next one won't miss," he growled again. The word "miss" came out as "meeess". Still Noonan held his ground. Then out of the corner of his eye, Noonan saw another blurry figure moving towards him through the trees. At first, he thought it might be his vision playing tricks on him, but the figure kept moving, a hovering silhouette. The figure quickly focussed into the distinct figure of a man. But who?

The figure stopped two feet behind Ackland and waited, poised. Noonan felt a trickle of excitement running down his spine. Perhaps there was another way out of this after all. Ackland raised the gun, aiming at a point at the centre of Noonan's head. Then the figure struck. He lifted his right leg and brought it down hard behind Ackland's right knee. At the same time, he thrust his left arm around Ackland's throat and grabbed the right wrist with his right hand. Ackland's body dropped to his knees. Noonan dived to the ground and rolled forward, out of a possible line of fire. Ackland grunted and swore in another language. Ackland's assailant began to throttle him with his left arm and a terrible gargling noise came from his throat. He pulled back Ackland's arm, wrestling with the gun. There was a flash of lightning as another shot popped off and rocketed across the night. Ackland's assailant pulled back the arm again and again, the gun quickly flying out of his hand and into the dark pools of shadow to the left.

Noonan got to his feet and rushed at Ackland, aiming two vicious blows to the Adams's apple, driving all the air out of his lungs. He retched and Noonan brought his foot viciously down onto Ackland's knees, forcing him to the ground. It was only then that Noonan looked up to see who his ally was. He immediately recognised Spanton's manically blazing eyes and curly, dark blond hair. Spanton was driving his right hand hard onto the back of Ackland's neck. Ackland was weakening dramatically. Then something shiny like a mirror suddenly appeared in his hand which drove upwards. Noonan's finely tuned reflexes saved him from a possibly fatal cut. He jumped backwards, missing the hunting knife by inches. Then suddenly Ackland was on his feet again, a terrible leer on his face and the flash of desperation in his eyes. He ran a few paces and then turned back to face Noonan and Spanton, slicing through the night air with the knife. His eyes moved like a caged animal's between Noonan and Spanton.

"He's mine," Noonan called out, the blood throbbing in his ears and the lust to kill proving too hard to resist. These were the moments he feared the most and were the source of all his nightmares. But for now, there was no turning back.

"If there's any left over, save some for me," came back Spanton's voice. Noonan moved carefully towards Ackland, his arms out in front of him. He could see the hatred in Ackland's eyes. When he was in range of the knife, Noonan suddenly dived to the floor and rolled again, coming up behind Ackland's knife. It all happened in less than two seconds and Ackland could barely follow him with his eyes. Noonan came in front of Ackland with his back to him. He grabbed Ackland's right wrist with both hands and brought his foot down hard on Ackland's toes. Ackland screamed out in pain. Noonan pulled Ackland's body down and threw him over his shoulder. He landed hard on the ground. Not wasting a second, Noonan drove his foot into Ackland's shoulder, clamping him to the ground. Then with both arms, he viciously snapped Ackland's arm out of its socket. The knife clattered uselessly to the ground and a terrible, piercing cry exploded from Ackland's lungs. Noonan brought his hand down hard on Ackland's throat and the sound prematurely cut out. Noonan reached over, grabbed the knife, and snapped it to Ackland's throat.

"Lomax made a mistake with you," Noonan told him quietly. "You just weren't up to the job." Then the knife came up and flashed down hard twice into Ackland's stomach. The heaving body sagged then and went limp. The head fell back. This time, rather than a sickness, Noonan felt a rush of electricity surging through his body. He wiped the knife on Ackland's shirt and shoved it into his pocket. Then slowly, his breathing became more even, and his heart rate returned to a normal pace. He was suddenly aware of Spanton's feet at his side.

Noonan looked up at Spanton and nodded gratefully. "Thanks," he said quietly.

"I've been watching that bastard all evening," Spanton replied. "He checked your room, saw that you weren't there, and he's been waiting around for you since. I've been waiting around with him." He paused. "You play your cards pretty close to the chest, Noonan, and I don't like it. What the hell were you doing out here?"

"I've got a girl, haven't I?" replied Noonan. "She hasn't seen me for about a month. She doesn't even know where the hell I am. There's a phone box in the village. I just wanted to talk to her, that's all." Spanton stared back at him, a suspicious and disbelieving look on his face. "Well, what's the matter, Spanton?" Noonan snapped. "Don't you have a girl around somewhere?"

"Not a girl, no," replied Spanton, shaking his head once. "And as it happens, I don't believe you. I think you're lying. What do you think I am, stupid? I don't know what you're up to, Noonan, but when I find out..." He let the threat hang in the cold night air.

They looked at each other for a long moment, sizing each other up. Then Noonan finally said, "We need to get rid of this guy right now." He looked around in the darkness, moved into the shadows, got down on his hands and knees and felt around in the damp undergrowth for the gun. It took around twenty seconds for his fingers to rub against the cold metal. He whipped it up and shoved it into his trousers. Spanton watched him, his hands in his overcoat pockets. Noonan looked around for any signs of blood, Spanton hanging back in the darkness. He found a small brown smudge of it on the mud. Noonan scuffed it with his boot until it had disappeared into the earth.

"I've been over every inch of this place," said Spanton. "There's a dry well on the other side of the estate. We can dump him down there. I suppose you've got something figured out for when Lomax comes back to find his loyal Golden Retriever missing. He's hardly likely to believe he's run off to join a monastery, is he?"

Noonan shrugged. "Worry about that later."

Spanton took the head and Noonan the feet. They jogged through the darkness. There was no moon and Noonan could only see a few feet in front of him. Spanton continued to give him directions, "left here, now go right", until they were right on the outer perimeter of the estate. Spanton suddenly gasped, "Stop here!" Noonan looked around, lowering the body behind him. He saw the round, circular wall of the dry well directly ahead of him.

"OK," Noonan called behind him. They picked up Ackland's body and manoeuvred it over the brick wall, feet first, until it was vertical. Then they let it go. The body dropped into black space. Noonan listened. He estimated that it was around eight seconds before he heard a dull plop and a splash. Noonan dropped the gun in after him and heard a much smaller plop and splash after about the same interval. In the darkness, unseen by Spanton, he slipped the knife into his sock. Something told him that it may be his last resort. He felt satisfied; even if Lomax suspected that the body was down there, he was going to have a job trying to retrieve it.

Spanton blew outwards. "Bastard weighs a ton."

They raced back to the track leading up to the house, which was still lit up as bright as day.

"How do you turn these damn things off?" Noonan snapped. They ran back along the track, Spanton looking to the left, Noonan to the right. Then Noonan saw it, a black iron post jutting out of the grass on the side. "Here!" he called to Spanton. There was a flap on top that Ackland had left open. There was a knob inside that Noonan twisted. The floodlights instantly snapped off and the track was plunged back into darkness again.

"Don't know what time Lomax is arriving back, but we'd better get some sleep. It's going to be a rough day," Noonan sighed wearily. Spanton just gave him one final, brutal look, then they moved back in the direction of the house. The front door was ajar, and they moved carefully inside. Noonan listened hard but heard nothing. In near-complete blackness, Noonan and Spanton felt their way back upstairs and into their rooms. Noonan looked at his watch. It was two o'clock in the morning. His body was warm and tingling with sweat. He was not sure he would be able to sleep but he had to try.

What a mess! Things couldn't have gone worse. He had not planned for the death of Ackland. Certainly, he had needed to be silenced, and he had taken great personal satisfaction in damaging Lomax's domestic security arrangements temporarily. But there would be a price to pay for his insurrection. And what of Spanton? For some reason, he had become an unlikely ally, albeit a distrusting one.

So, first Brewster and now Spanton. In the face of adversity, they were reluctantly coming together as a team.

Ackland had been a satisfying kill. He had even enjoyed it, which bothered him. He thought of Jarrett then; the void had swallowed him long before Noonan had known him. It could easily happen to Noonan too. If only he could get back to Anna, he would be safe. He closed his eyes and willed sleep to take him away. Slowly, painfully slowly, sleep lapped at his feet, then covered him whole...

... And then he was back on Mr Burton's farm again, looking for Jarrett's grave. He felt as if he had been there a thousand times before but still, he knew not whether the grave was intact. He crashed through the dark forest, the wind blowing fiercely into his face. It was blowing so hard it was becoming hard to move forward. The leaves on the trees felt like knives as they whipped at his face. Then suddenly he had broken free of the forest, and he was standing before Jarrett's grave; and, just as he had feared, it was empty.

191

"Noonan!" The voice cracked like a whip from out of the forest. Noonan wheeled around, terror gripping him like a cold hand around the throat. He knew that voice. It was Lomax's voice. Lomax came striding out of the forest, gliding almost, frighteningly quickly, his face white and his eyes black. "Noonan!" he barked again.

Then Noonan awoke with a start and realised that he was not dreaming. Lomax was leaning into him, his arm pressing into Noonan's neck, his black, accusing eyes burning into him like a judge handing down a sentence of death. Noonan felt the nauseous sensation of drowning as his air supply was cut off. His body instantly snapped into action, pushing against Lomax, and twisting to get out of the hold he was in. He had known this was coming, but not as early as this. It was not yet light outside.

"Where's Ackland?" he asked quietly, almost with a kind curiosity, like a doctor asking a patient if they had been suffering from any known symptoms. Noonan stared defiantly back, saying nothing, pressing the fear that was welling up in his stomach firmly back into place.

192

Noonan felt the struggle begin to seep out of him. He choked and gasped.

"Ackland was a fool for letting himself get taken by you. But he was my man!" Lomax growled. His right fist came down onto Noonan's Adam's apple. Noonan choked, tried to roll out of the bed, but only made it to the edge before Lomax pulled him back and brought his enormous fist down hard on the same spot again. An explosion of pain ripped across Noonan's chest and his stomach tried to force phlegm up into his throat. He coughed it back. With all the strength that he could summon, Noonan rolled to the edge of the bed again and this time managed to fall onto the floor. He instantly spun onto his back, coiled back his legs, and then thrust them forward. Lomax jumped up from the bed and leaned down. Noonan's feet connected with Lomax's head, pushing his body back into the room. Noonan groggily got to his feet, but Lomax was already coming back at him, and Noonan, still experiencing the waves of nausea and disorientation, was unable to stop the lightning fast blows that Lomax was now delivering hard into his ribs. Noonan felt himself being driven into the far corner of

193

the tiny room. His body connected with the wall and his mind instantly cleared; he had to fight Lomax with everything that he had left. All the confused emotions of anger, terror and hatred became entangled in his heart and Noonan began to fight back at Lomax with a desperate, final intensity, the likes of which he had never experienced before.

He dived forward on the balls of his feet, delivering two ferocious blows to the side of Lomax's head. He may as well have been hitting out a stone gargoyle. Lomax ducked the next few blows that Noonan aimed at him, then came back at him, shooting forward with his arms. The blows seemed to penetrate Noonan's chin and go straight through him. Noonan felt consciousness seeping out of him. He felt Lomax grabbing him and twisting him round. Then he felt his huge hand clamping around his throat and squeezing. It only took a few seconds. Noonan felt consciousness slipping quickly away from him and his body quickly dropping to the floor. The blackness opened above him and quickly swallowed him whole. He surrendered willingly to it, floating into a void where he knew there would no longer be any more pain...

Life clung obstinately onto Noonan. He had been ready to leave it all behind and peer behind the curtain of the next life. Perhaps he would find Anna there. But as he opened his eyes and smelled the musty, damp smell of the cellar, he knew he was back in the world he remembered. It was almost completely dark in the cellar, with just a pinprick of light shining in through a crack in the wall from outside. He painfully lifted himself to his elbows, pain shooting through his body. He gasped in agony. Painfully, he crawled forward on his side until he felt his head hitting a wall. He spun slowly round and gently lowered himself to the floor, resting his back against the wall. His breathing came out slowly, evenly. His body fell slightly to the right and rubbed against something soft and warm. He was about to withdraw sharply away, then realised that he was not alone in the cellar; Brewster was sitting right next to him, perched against the wall.

"Is that you, Noonan?" his voice echoed in the darkness.

"It's me," Noonan replied, his voice little more than a painful gasp.

"I didn't think I'd be seeing you down here."

"I didn't think I'd be seeing you," Noonan replied simply.   There was not much more to say.   The two men sat in the darkness, finding comfort in the sound of each other's breathing.

"What the hell happened to you?"

"I tried to get out, didn't I?"

"Thought you weren't going to try that."

"Yesterday evening I wasn't going to."   They were quiet for a moment. Noonan's neck ached and he closed his eyes for a second.   "Ackland's dead."

"You?"

"That's right."

"So, that just leaves Lomax, then. After the job, Noonan, we take him, right?"

Noonan thought about everything that had happened over the course of the evening and what Lomax had done to them.

"Yeah," Noonan replied, his voice a soft echo. "We take him." He felt a dry itch in his throat. "What the hell happened to you, Brewster?"

"What do you care?"

"I'm just interested, I guess."

"I was getting out with my girl, Jean. I had it all worked out. The flight, the passports, everything. Only when I got to her place, they'd killed her. My boss's orders. And now he's after me. The rest of it you know." He paused. "So, what's your story, Noonan?"

"I had a girl too. I might have married her. But now Lomax has her."

"What's her name?"

"Anna."

"Anna..." Brewster seemed to be processing the name. There was plenty of dust in the cellar and Brewster coughed. "Noonan?"

"Yeah?"

"Lomax has got all my money. But he didn't get our passports. I've still got them on me."

"So?"

"We could get Lomax inside the bank and then make our own way out. I know a place where we can hole up. After that, when the heat cools off, it's up to you what you do. But I'm out of here, out of the country. What do you say?"

"It won't do any good. Interpol will pick you up the moment you try to walk through customs. Lomax would have already thought of that."

"But in my case, they'll be looking for John Brewster. John Davidson will slip right past them." He paused. "That's the name on the passport. Jean was to be Susan Farmer."

Noonan chuckled for a second. "With your skills you should have been working for Lomax. Or I could have been doing what you're doing."

"Yeah," Brewster sighed. "And we'd still have ended up down here,

198

without our girls." He paused. "Well, what do you think?"

"It could work - if we make it out of there."

"Yeah. If we make it out of there." He paused again. "Just one thing though: if things are looking bad, don't leave me in that bank. You got that, Noonan?"

Noonan exhaled slowly. "Yeah," he replied. "I've got that."

15

The rainswept London Street lit up like a mirror under the harsh glare of twin headlights as the Harrods lorry went on its way. The February drizzle floated in the dark night sky before settling on the wet tarmac. It was a dreary, depressing evening, wrapping up in one unattractive package everything that made February no-one's favourite month of the year. A single lamp post lit the street on one side. A young couple came tripping merrily along the damp pavement and passed under it, the girl, blond, wide-eyed, and laughing, wrapped up luxuriously in a white mink coat. Her partner, a young man in thick black spectacles, with thick black hair covering his ears and hanging past his collar, was smiling contentedly. Then just as quickly as they had appeared in the light, the shadows quickly swallowed them up again.

Nothing then moved on the street. Light from a gallery at the far end of the street shone out, a modern, somewhat jazzy piece of work displayed in the window for all to see. Then five silhouettes, all dressed in black overalls, emerged from the shadows. It would have been hard for anyone, had they been watching from the other side of the street, to know how long they had been hiding there. They darted through the shadows towards the gallery lit up at the end of the street.

Noonan, second in the line, was watching Lomax's back as he led them towards their target. The cold, wet evening was at least keeping people off the street. Lomax darted into a thin alley by the side of the gallery. Noonan followed and felt the other three move in behind him. They waited in a line, watching, and listening carefully. All five carried rucksacks on their backs. They took black balaclavas out of their back pockets and pulled them down over their faces, leaving them as luminous, round spheres peering out of the shadows.

Spanton reached into his rucksack, pulling out a coiled length of rope and a steel hook. He tied the hook to the end of the rope and looked back at the others. Understanding his silent instruction, they inched away, giving him room, and crouching down in the shadows. Spanton stood erect and alert for a few seconds. The quiet hiss of a car sounded from the street, briefly throwing bright light onto the edge of the alley. Unconsciously, Noonan felt himself crouching lower down. Then the car passed on and droned away into the night. Noonan felt Katharina's arm pressing into his. Spanton's body coiled like a panther ready to pounce, his head craning upwards like an animal listening for its prey. Then, in a flash of movement, Spanton's body sprang. The hook shot upwards like a missile. There was a brief clatter of metal on masonry and then Spanton was pulling the rope taut. He shot up the wall like a monkey, his arms racing to get ahead, his feet virtually tripping up the wall. Then his body was at the top and heaving itself over. His legs showed for a moment and then he was gone. A minute passed in thick silence before a brief whistling sound came from above, which Noonan took to be the signal.

202

He moved forward noiselessly and grabbed the rope. Just then, a loud cough rang out and he ducked down into the shadows again. An old drunk in a beige overcoat, swinging a bottle in a brown paper bag, was standing at the entrance of the alley. He coughed and wheezed and spluttered. Then with a satisfied belch the old man staggered on, his scuffling footsteps fading into the distance. Noonan heaved his body up and, hand over hand, scaled the wall. His rubber shoes gripped the wet wall firmly enough. Then he was at the top and heaving himself over.

Spanton was waiting with the rope around his waist. Noonan added his weight to it. After a minute, Katharina's head appeared at the edge and, raising her legs behind her, she somersaulted gracefully over the top, coming down gently onto the gravel top. Brewster came next, cursing loudly as he pulled himself over. He looked remarkably undamaged considering what he had been through. Noonan himself only felt a slight pinch of pain on the right-hand side of his face if he moved his facial muscles too quickly. In no time at all, Lomax had hauled himself onto the roof. He pointed to a tall building ahead of them, a block of offices, twenty metres higher than the one they were on.

Spanton allowed himself a grin of anticipation. He appeared to be enjoying himself. He ran in a crouch to the other end of the roof, crouched again, swung the rope with the metal hook attached and let it soar upward into the night sky. There following the distant, familiar clang of the hook as it gripped the edge of the roof high up in the air. And then Spanton was swinging towards the building and rapidly ascending it. His feet occasionally slipped on the wet masonry, but he maintained his footing and scrambled to the top. They maintained the same order on the second ascent. Noonan positioned himself at the edge of the roof as Spanton swung the rope towards him. He stood up on the small wall, gripped the rope and let himself go into black, wet, empty space. A second later his boots hit the taller building and he immediately started to heave himself up. He noticed with some irritation that the rain was starting to come down heavier. He watched the bricks in the wall going past, and concentrated fiercely: left hand, right hand, left foot, right foot, and again, and again... He was a machine.

Nothing could happen to him now. His shoulder ached but then with a final effort, he pulled himself to the top, over the edge, and collapsed down against the wall.

"Well done, old man." Spanton voice was lined with sarcasm. Noonan glanced at him but said nothing. He wondered if Spender would already have the entire area covered with police, who would not be easily visible, tucked away in the dark shadows of the surrounding streets. Noonan forced Spender from his mind. There was nothing he could do about him right now. There was no going back.

Over the course of ten minutes the other three made it to the top of the roof. Lomax pointed to the opposite end of the roof. "Next roof," he said, looking straight ahead. They ran silently to the other end. The adjacent roof was the same height and six feet away. It would have to be jumped. Spanton climbed onto the edge and threw his body forward. His feet clipped the edge of the building and he pitched forward, rolling into the darkness. It was Noonan's turn. He stepped up onto the roof's edge without looking down. He measured the distance in front of him and leapt. His heart missed a beat, but then his right foot hit the edge and he rolled forward onto the gravelled roof. He moved back to the edge. Katharina's body wobbled as she climbed onto the edge, and he could see for the first-time genuine terror in her eyes. She braced herself and flung her body forward. Her foot landed on the edge, but her body wobbled again, then started to rock backwards. Katharina let out a squawk of terror, but Noonan had already grabbed her waist with both arms. He pulled her over to safety.

"Thanks," she breathed heavily, her voice shaking with shock. Noonan gently let her go. He waited, poised for Brewster, who made it over without a problem. He paid Lomax no attention but heard his feet crunch onto the gravel a few seconds later.

A distant rumble spread across the night sky and a thick shaft of light seemed to be casting around in the darkness like a giant eye. A small structure stood at one corner of the roof with a door in its centre, leading down into the building.

"Down!" hissed Lomax. They all dived to the ground, pressing themselves against the wall. The throbbing engines of the helicopter increased in volume and Noonan felt his heart pounding hard against the gravel. Was the helicopter one of Spender's? It was certainly possible. He felt horribly exposed and screwed his eyes tight shut. The engines of the helicopter were getting nearer, their remorseless throb growing louder... Louder... *Louder...*

16

Noonan felt the jagged pebbles on the roof cutting into his forehead as the seconds ticked away. But quickly the ferocious chug of the helicopter passed over them and diminished, moving away until it became a distant growl. Noonan looked up. Lomax and Brewster were already on their feet. He slowly stood up.

Lomax looked intensely at them. "Alright then," he murmured with grim intent. Then he was already moving towards the structure in the corner of the building. The door was made of thick steel with a Yale lock underneath the slim handle. They all crowded around the door.

"Blow it," Lomax ordered Katharina. Noonan found himself kneeling on the gravel with the others as Katharina reached into her rucksack. In the darkness he could see her pulling out a steel box and a thin coil. Lomax switched on a pencil torch which threw a tiny circle of light on the lock. Noonan watched as she took out a handful of plastic explosives from the box and covered the lock with a small amount of it. Noonan could not see the colour, but he assumed it to be Semtex. She then stuck the end of the coil into the middle of it, measuring with her mind, and slicing the end off with a penknife. She took out a lighter from the pocket of her overalls, looked up at the light rain, and a flame snapped upwards from the lighter. She lit the end of the coil and moved backwards sharply. They all lowered themselves onto their stomachs and Noonan covered his ears with his fingers. Through his muffled ears he could hear the explosion twenty seconds later, which still sounded shockingly loud. He looked up, removing his fingers from his ears. An ugly black gash had been torn into a section of the door and billows of smoke were pouring out on to the rooftop.

They got to their feet and approached the door. Lomax, fiddling his fingers into a pair of gloves, gently pulled at the door, which would have been scorching hot. The handle had completely disappeared. The door made a groaning sound as Lomax pulled it back. He beckoned the others inside and they followed.

Lomax's pencil torch danced around the walls. They were in a stairwell with their feet clanging softly on metal steps. Green signs on the walls told them that they were in a Fire Escape. They moved softly down the staircase, their rubber shoes treading delicately on the metal, their breathing low and controlled, as if the very staircase was a living being that might awake with a start at the slightest sound. Noonan, at the back of the line, counted four floors before they reached the ground. There was a faint smell of fresh paint in the air. Lomax, at the front, kept his pencil torch steady. There was a plain white door to the side leading into the main body of the building. Lomax pointed the torch over Brewster's head and held up three fingers to him. "Three minutes," he mouthed to him urgently. Brewster eyed him coldly and nodded. He took a small roll of fabric from his rucksack. Lomax reached into his bag, took out a small circular device and handed the torch to

Brewster. He pressed a button on the side of the device and a series of red LED numbers flashed up in the centre, throwing red light on each of their faces. Quickly Lomax set the timer to three minutes. The numbers immediately started to drip away: 3:00, 2:59, 2:58... Silently, Lomax pushed the handle down and pushed. There was a quiet squeak as the door opened. The five of them rushed in.

Brewster immediately shone the torch down towards the ground where a metal grid in the wall was positioned by the door. He knelt at the grid, which was held together by four screws. Brewster instantly handed the torch back to Lomax, who held the beam firmly on the grid. Brewster unravelled the fabric, which contained a collection of tools. He selected a screwdriver with the correct end and began to work on the four screws. Quickly the cover came away. The others knelt behind him. Noonan understood the significance of the three-minute time limit. The grid in the wall housed a sophisticated alarm system which would have picked up their presence in the main banking room. They had three minutes to disable the system before it sounded out in the local police station. Noonan looked down into the grid, which seemed to be made up of a complicated series of wires all plugged into different sockets. There was a red light showing in the top right-hand corner. Brewster took out a sheet of paper from his pocket and began to feverishly refer to it. It was a diagram drawn in pencil with various lines going off to a series of letters and numbers. Brewster started pulling out various wires and hurriedly rearranging them. Noonan glanced at the stopwatch: 2:20. 2:19, 2:18...

Noonan had no hope of being able to follow what Brewster was doing, but his movements were fiercely precise and controlled. The only sign of stress on Brewster's face was a single line of sweat that had started to form on the top of his forehead. He looked at Lomax, whose facial muscles had tautened. His eyes bored into the alarm system, willing it to comply to his wishes. Brewster cursed silently and removed some of the wires that he had just put in. Time bled slowly and inexorably away from them. Spanton's eyes twitched excitedly;

Katharina pressed her lips into a bloodless line.

1:30, 1:29, 1:28...

Brewster continued to work in a controlled frenzy. The silence burned into Noonan's ears. A single drop of sweat ran down Brewster's forehead. Noonan felt his breath coming out smoothly, evenly, and he put his mind into neutral.

0:28, 0:27, 0:26...

Noonan felt his heartbeat begin to quicken. Still Brewster kept working furiously. Noonan pushed his lips together.

0:10, 0:09. 0:08...

"For God's sake, Brewster!" hissed Lomax.

0:02.

Brewster suddenly took his hands away. The red light went out and a green light immediately underneath it snapped on with a soft *bleep* sound.

0:01. 0:00.

Brewster turned to Lomax and nodded. Noonan let his breath out in a long sigh. They all raised themselves to full height.

Lomax shone his torch into the large, cavernous, palatial room that on quick inspection revealed itself to be the main banking room. The floor was of shiny marble with a black and grey design. A row of service desks behind thick glass, ten in all, were spaced evenly along the furthest wall. Ten blinds hung obstinately down over the glass. It had been close of business for over five hours now and the rush of hurried feet out into the streets of Knightsbridge had long since departed. In the middle of the day the room would have been bustling with activity, bodies lined up in a snaking queue to get to the service desks, the murmur of voices hanging like a fog in the air. Now, the room was eerie in its silence, foreboding in its vastness. A row of red ropes lined the centre of the room for the customers to queue up in an orderly fashion. At the far end of the room was a magnificent mahogany door stretching up to the ceiling. Lomax pointed to Brewster and silently indicated to it.

They moved cautiously through the expansive room. In their black overalls and black balaclavas, they were moving shadows. Noonan felt like he was walking quietly through a silent cathedral. They got to the door and Brewster reached up with his gloved hand, pulling the handle down. The door groaned open. Lomax shone his torch into another tall, expansive room, lined with desks and typewriters. A thick red carpet stretched out across the floor. It could have been a room in any office anywhere. At the far end was a solid wooden door with a single pane of rectangular glass which led down to the vaults and the safety deposit boxes. There was only one more door to get past. Lomax indicated to the others to stand completely still on the wooden partition separating the two rooms. According to Lomax, one section under the carpet had a pressure pad wired to an alarm that would sound in the street. The only way to get safely across the carpet was to knock out the alarm. Lomax pointed the torch up to a black box on the wall close to the ceiling. Noonan cupped his palms together and Brewster placed his foot on them. Lomax held the door steady. Noonan lifted Brewster upwards. Brewster's fingers

215

gripped the top of the door. He placed his right foot on the door handle and manoeuvred his way round the door. On the other side, Brewster placed his two feet on a ledge halfway up the wall and took out his roll of tools. He gripped the black box and straightened himself up. With the pencil torch stuffed in his mouth, Brewster lifted the lid and squinted at the wires inside. He gently, almost lovingly stroked the wires inside and explored them with his fingers right up to the sockets. Then he delicately removed a pair of pliers and, like a surgeon, working from the top, snipped the ends of all the wires. He jumped down. The other four streamed into the room.

They moved quickly to the wooden door. Katharina quickly took her rucksack from her back and examined the lock in front of her. She pressed her finger into the aperture and calculated again. She took the Semtex out of her bag. It had to be just the right amount: too little would just make a mess of the door, too much could take out the staircase beyond and blow the splinters backwards and into them. She carefully measured out the correct amount of Semtex and gently filled

216

the lock with it.   She took out the coil, stuck one end in and, stepping backwards carefully, unspooled the thin wire until eight feet of it hung tautly in the air. She took cover behind the nearest desk and the others crowded in around her.   She handed them pieces of wax which they stuffed into their ears.   She took out the lighter and lit the wire.   It sparked, caught, and crackled, shooting up the wire towards the lock. Katharina leaned in, her forehead touching her knee.

Three seconds, she counted.

Two...

One...

The explosion ripped through the room, shooting splinters across like bullets which sailed harmlessly over their heads. Katharina waited a couple of seconds and cautiously lifted her head. A chunk of the door around the keyhole had disappeared leaving a black, gaping wound.   She quickly removed the wax and moved to the door, the others following. Lomax pushed past her and ripped the remains of the door back. He switched the torch on. A wooden staircase led underground.   He gestured impatiently   for   the   others   to   follow.

Noonan followed the back of Lomax's head as he led them down the spiral staircase. At the bottom, a door with bars blocked their way forward. They lined up in a row, peering through the bars. Lomax shone the torch through. The circle of light hit upon row upon row of safety deposit boxes.

Noonan felt his pulse quickening. They were nearing the end of their journey.

17

It took ten minutes for Katharina to finish setting up the final explosion that would enable them to break into the vault. The five of them pressed their backs into the wall, their knees up to their chins, the wax back in their ears.

The explosion ripped through the underground room, sending the bars of the door flying backwards towards the staircase. The foundations of the building seemed to rock, and a section of the roof came crashing down to the floor, missing them by inches. Then they were suddenly choking and spluttering in a thick fog of dust and smoke, all vision suddenly lost. Noonan felt the debris penetrating his lungs and a wave of nausea passed over him. He screwed his eyes tight shut and, despite the wax, his ears were ringing sharply. He felt Lomax getting up beside him. He was waving his hands around frantically, desperately trying to fan the smoke away. Slowly it cleared to reveal the extent of the damage: the door had completely disappeared, and the surrounding bars were sticking out at wild, demented angles. The ends were sharp as knives. The roof of the vault had become blackened, and the safety deposit boxes nearest the door had suffered the ferocity of the blast. A white haze hung in the air. They got to their feet and carefully entered the vault. The boxes felt scorching hot.

"You sure you used enough of that stuff?" Spanton sneered at Katharina, who appeared not to hear him.

Lomax looked at his watch and started down the long line of boxes, rising to the ceiling, all with different numbers on them. "Right," he barked at them. "Start loading them." The four of them looked at each other, as if unsure where to start. Finally, Spanton made a move, pulling the rucksack from his back and ripping at the boxes nearest to him. This seemed to snap the others into action, and they quickly followed his lead, grabbing them and loading them into the rucksacks. Noonan worked deliberately slowly, looking around him. He watched as Lomax's eyes darted like a hungry wolf, up and down the rows of boxes, a wild, deranged look on his face. The insanity of the man was suddenly boiling over; Noonan felt the cold hand of fear seize him suddenly. Noonan knew that look only too well. These were the moments when Lomax was capable of anything. His mouth was moving up and down in a strange chant, though Noonan assumed that he was merely reading the numbers and looking for the right one. He appeared to have forgotten all about the rest of them. *The* box was the only thing in the world that mattered. Noonan was watching him, both fascinated and sickened in equal measure.

Towards the wall at the end, he suddenly froze and let out an animal-like yelp of exhilaration; he had found it. He drove back his arm and with a cry drove it forward, his fist bunched into a ball, smashing through the lock with the power of a human bulldozer. The lock came free, and Lomax ripped it out by the handle on the end. Noonan looked at the shiny metal box, one foot wide and two and half feet deep.

All the secrets of the world...

"Are those the diamonds?" Spanton asked, crouched down, his hand gripping a deposit box, his eyes wide, sounding almost like a child.

Lomax turned to them, his eyes still blazing with a frightening intensity. A gun, a Browning .9mm had magically appeared in his hand. "Get over here, all of you," he said with a quiet deadliness.

"What about the diamonds?" Spanton demanded. "I want to see inside that box!"

"I don't think we were ever supposed to," Brewster said bitterly.

Lomax turned the gun on Brewster, and it flashed nastily. "One more word..." he warned him. Noonan was numb. Deep down, he had always known that it would end like this. It had to. But he had gone along with the whole thing and played it straight down the line. For himself. For Anna. If none of them were to make it out of the bank, he could only hope that Spender was in position outside, ready to grab Lomax the moment he tried to leave the bank. But right now, it looked like

222

there was no way out for the rest of them. Everything he had worked for, everything he had done – it had to mean *something.* Noonan felt the blood draining from his head. Spanton was still wailing and Brewster cursing. Katharina had remained silent, the cogs in her head working smoothly.

"Get over here, all of you," Lomax warned them finally. "This is it. Your last chance. Or I'll drop you right here."

"Do as he says," Noonan murmured from the corner of his mouth.

"Shut up!" Lomax barked, the gun swinging round to Noonan.

The four of them shuffled like zombies towards Lomax at the back of the vault. They formed in a line in front of him. Noonan looked down it. At the end, Spanton's face had reddened, and he was glowering ferociously at Lomax. Brewster and Katharina were both looking directly back at Noonan, as though trying to read his mind. Brewster's face was taut, his eyes telling Noonan that he was ready to move at the slightest signal. Katharina appeared to be mouthing something at him, but Noonan could make no sense of it. Seconds ticked endlessly by.

Lomax smiled icily. "Goodbye," he said simply.

And then Spanton, at the end of the line, suddenly let out a wild scream. He dived at Lomax, his hands reaching desperately for the gun. It was a futile gesture, born out of irrepressible rage and terrible desperation. Yet it bought Noonan that splinter of a second that he needed to spring into action. Lomax brought the gun up and fired instantaneously at Spanton's leaping body. The explosive sound of the gun was shockingly loud in the confined space. The bullet ripped open a hole in Spanton's chest and his body dropped awkwardly to the ground, a dark, wet stain spreading across his overalls. Brewster, Noonan, and Katharina dived into Lomax less than a second later. Fighting for space, Noonan brought his hand down furiously on Lomax's trachea. But he may have been hacking away at stone. Katharina punched repeatedly at his head and Brewster went for the gun. They wrestled with it, Brewster desperately trying to prise it out of his hand, but Lomax's

strength was considerably greater. The
ugly snout of the automatic found its way
round to Brewster and it flashed its deadly
orange flame, barking loudly. The bullet
tore into the side of Brewster's stomach,
and his body fell limply backwards.
Noonan's hand went for the knife in his
boot, and he ripped it out, but Lomax
quickly knocked it from his hand. It
landed close to Brewster's body. Instead,
Noonan brought his foot up and kicked out
viciously at Lomax's hand, sending the gun
flying across the room. Katharina and
Noonan watched the gun, both having the
same thought at the same moment.
Momentarily, forgetting Lomax, both flung
their bodies forward in a desperate bid to
get to the gun. Noonan got there first,
slamming his fingers round the butt, and
jumping up, spinning his body round in the
air as he did so. Katharina's body
slammed into his, her fingers clawing at
the gun. Noonan pushed her away with
his left hand and pointed the gun at
Lomax. Lomax, the box wrapped in his
arms, was rushing towards Noonan. He
stopped when he saw the gun pointing
steadily in his direction. His eyes sparkled
in deadly amusement, as if the unexpected
development was all part of some crazy,

225

existential joke. For a moment everything froze.

Then Katharina's voice cut through the dark, dusty room. "Kill him," she said in a hard voice. Noonan kept the gun on Lomax. "Kill him!" she repeated more urgently.

"He won't," Lomax sneered. "He can't. Because he knows he'll never be free if he does."

"Then let me do it!" she snapped.
"I don't doubt you would," Noonan replied quickly. Then back at Lomax: "Where's Anna?"

Lomax just stared back at him, his eyes revealing nothing. The distant sound of two-tone police sirens suddenly filled the air, getting closer.

"We're running out of time, Noonan!" Katharina's voice cut in.

"Where's Anna?" Noonan repeated, his finger tightening on the trigger.

The sound of the front doors being broken down outside cut through to the basement. Unseen by none of them, Brewster's bloodied hand had reached down to grasp the knife that Noonan had dropped and lifted it. The knife flashed in the darkened room.

"You can't win, Noonan," Lomax sneered, smiling coldly.

The knife flashed, driving upwards into Lomax's shin. Lomax momentarily cried out, the safety deposit box tumbling out of his hands and landing on the floor with a sharp clatter. In a state of fury, Brewster tried to lift the knife and sink the knife into the shin a second time, but the effort proved too much, and he fell backwards, losing consciousness. Lomax dropped to his knees. His hands grabbed for the box, but Katharina got to it first, swiftly picking it up. She raised her boot and drove it viciously into Lomax's face. Blood poured from his nose, and he looked wildly around. Katharina turned to Noonan, furiously determined. "LET'S GET THE HELL OUT OF HERE!" she shouted.

Noonan looked down at Lomax. Blood was pouring out of the wound in his shin and from his nose. He was trying to raise himself to his knees. He was half-gasping in pain, half-laughing at the situation he found himself in. This was the moment Noonan had waited for, the moment he had talked of with Brewster, the moment when he was suddenly completely vulnerable and could be taken. But Noonan could not shoot, not while Lomax was still holding the missing piece of the jigsaw. Noonan turned to Brewster's bleeding body. He could see that Spanton, lying perfectly still against the wall of deposit boxes, was beyond help, Lomax's bullet having killed him instantly at point blank range. But Brewster was still breathing and could be saved. The bullet had torn through his side and probably hit his ribcage. Lomax was crawling snake-like towards them across the floor, his arm reaching up for the box. Noonan moved towards him.

"What are you doing?" Katharina yelled.

"I'm taking the bastard with me!" Noonan bellowed back, moving in on Lomax. The hammering on the main doors continued outside. Then everything went crazy. With a whistle of hydraulics, a steel cage door roared down from the ceiling. Noonan's body reacted instantaneously, and he spun backwards

228

on his heel, diving for safety. The huge cage crashed into position at the exact point where Noonan's body had been less than a second ago, separating Noonan from Lomax. Flashing alarm lights painted everything around them in a hellish red. Noonan rushed to the cage, pressing his face against the bars. Lomax's grimacing face was looking up at him. He was cackling sadistically. Noonan spat with disgust. For the moment, Lomax had won. Again.

Noonan ran for the door, jumping over the deposit boxes that lay scattered untidily across the floor. Katharina ran alongside him and tried to overtake him, but instead she ran straight into the snout of the gun, now pointing at her. Noonan had stopped and was indicating to Brewster's prone body a few feet away with his eyes.

"Help me pick him up," he ordered her. "He's coming with us!"

"Are you crazy?" she spat back with disgust. Nonetheless, not wanting to waste a second, she bent down to help Brewster up. Noonan took his other side, and they lifted him to his feet. Brewster was leaning into Noonan, trying to say something.

"Yeah, I know!" Noonan barked, not needing to hear it. He picked up the safety deposit box with his other hand. They shuffled their way desperately out of the vault, helping Brewster awkwardly up the steps. Noonan shoved the gun into the pocket of his overalls.

They raced as fast as they could back through the main banking room and up the stairs. They continued the steady climb to the roof. The hammering on the front doors intensified and quickly became unbearable. Noonan felt as though the sound was reverberating through his head like a terrible migraine. Next to him Brewster's breathing was coming out in sharp stabs, and he could feel his warm breath on the side of his face. Every step up the endless fire escape to the roof seemed to take a huge effort of will for all three of them. Noonan counted every terrible step to focus his mind. After what seemed like an age, they made it to halfway point. And it was then that the doors of the Central Bank in Knightsbridge suddenly exploded inwards and a small army of uniformed policemen

230

came swarming into the main banking
room...

18

Noonan felt Brewster's body rubbing against his as he made his way up the stairs. With every step it felt as though there was a force pushing him backwards. He pulled Brewster's arm around his shoulders and gripped it with his right arm clamped across his chest. In his left hand he gripped the safety deposit box, which bashed repeatedly against his left leg. The staircase twisted one final time and he saw the door leading onto the roof. Downstairs he could hear boots crashing on the metal stairs.

"Move!" he hissed through clench teeth. "They're coming!" Beside him he could hear Brewster giving out low moans as they hauled him up the last of the stairs. They crashed through the charred door and Noonan looked quickly to the side of the building leading in the opposite direction from the way they had come in. "This way!" Katharina did not protest. In the sky, a single light swung around for them. The helicopter was back.

They got to the edge and looked over. The roof of a block of luxury apartments lay in shadows ten feet below them. There was a two-foot gap between the buildings. Noonan looked at Katharina.

"Go!" he ordered her. She automatically stepped onto the edge and jumped into darkness. Noonan heard her feet crunch onto gravel. "Can you make it?" he asked Brewster.

"Yeah," he gasped painfully. Noonan helped him to the edge and pushed him hard. Then, not wasting a second, he climbed up and threw the box into the blackness, hearing it crunch onto the gravel. He followed it into the darkness a moment later. It seemed to take a few seconds but eventually his feet hit soft gravel and he felt his body twist as he straightened up. He helped Brewster to his feet. The thud of music throbbed up through the roof. An insistent drumbeat struck out like a metronome across the night. A small flight of stone steps disappeared into the building in the centre of the roof. Noonan desperately felt around for the box, but the pools of blackness kept it well hidden. Very quickly he felt his fingers brush against the sharp metal, and he scooped it up by the handle. With Katharina taking his other side, they dragged Brewster towards the pit of darkness and disappeared into it. In the blackness, Noonan carefully felt around for the steps. There were ten and beyond it, a door leading into the corridor of the top floor. Then the chug of the helicopter increased and throbbed into his ears. Katharina, Brewster, and Noonan crouched down at the corner of the door as the rectangle above them filled with bright light. The rumble of the helicopter filled Noonan's ears with its terrible cacophony and the rectangle suddenly blazed like a bolt from Heaven. Noonan squeezed himself tight into the corner pulling Brewster with him. And then a second later, the light in the rectangle snapped out and the helicopter was moving away, the terrible rumble in the sky gradually receding.

Noonan hurriedly examined the door in front of him. There was no light to see by, so he felt with his heads. He found the iron door handle and wrenched at it, but the door was frozen solid. He felt smooth, icy glass to the right of it. Instinctively he reached into his overalls and pulled out Lomax's pistol.

"Get back!" he hissed. He felt them drawing back. He raised the pistol and smashed at the glass with the butt. It was tough, thick glass but after several attempts the glass eventually gave way. The loud music thudding through from below provided adequate cover for the sound of breaking glass. Knocking out all jagged shards, Noonan reached his arm through and twisted the lock on the other side of the door. He pushed against it and the door swung open. It was pitch black inside the building and Noonan blinked to adjust his eyes to the darkness. The crashing music bled into his ears. The floor was carpeted, and Noonan felt the shattered glass crunch and pop as he stepped over it. A staircase led downwards. He bent down, lifting Brewster to his feet, and moved forward carefully. Brewster's body felt warm and

235

slimy against him, and Noonan realised that he was feeling blood against his fingers. Katharina was taking Brewster's other side. As they worked their way down the stairs a pool of murky light opened in front of them, and they soon came to a landing. They were on the top floor of a luxury block of flats. The door directly in front of them had the number twelve on the door. A piece of the "2" had broken off. The crashing music was sounding from behind this door and was now accompanied by the cacophony of loud voices and occasional braying laughter. Noonan hurried past quickly, worried that the door would burst open, and they would all be caught guiltily framed in it. The doors to flats 9, 10 and 11 stretched away down a corridor to the left. Beyond it was a staircase leading down. They took this as quickly as possible, Noonan looking anxiously around all the time as they worked their way down.

On the next floor down, a loud "ting!" suddenly sounded and a white arrow lit up above the grey metallic door of a lift. Noonan let Brewster's body drop gently to the floor and dived towards the lift. The door slid gently open with a whoosh and Noonan had the brief impression of a young face with tangled black, curly hair stepping out swinging a green bottle. Noonan cursed silently; he had no choice. He lifted his arm and drove his fist hard into his face. He felt the body fall backwards into the lift and heard the bottle crashing to the floor. He checked his pulse and carefully placed the body on the lift floor by the young man's sprawled legs. Noonan turned and looked at Katharina's face, glistening with tension. He raced back to her and picked up Brewster again. They hurriedly carried him into the lift, gently placing him down next to the unconscious young man. Noonan jabbed repeatedly at the button for the underground car park. The lift wheezed into action and glided to a halt seconds later. The metallic doors hissed open.

Cool air hit Noonan's forehead and he smelled the mustiness of the underground car park. They stepped carefully over the unconscious young man. Noonan hit the top floor button to send him on his way, and they stepped carefully out into the car park. They were confronted by an assortment of expensive vehicles that looked like they were lined up in a car showroom. Noonan assumed that some of these cars belonged to the guests at the party. The lift doors sighed shut and it wheezed upwards. A white Mercedes was parked prominently at the end of a row.

"Can you get one of these going?" Noonan asked Katharina. She shrugged and moved carefully through the darkness, peering into each of the vehicles. She stopped at the Mercedes on the end and nodded at Noonan. She looked around quickly, then dropped to her knee. Noonan could see her in the shadows working on the lock. After what seemed like two minutes, she pulled the passenger door open and crawled into the car.

Noonan looked down into Brewster's face, which had become pallid and grey. A deathly sheen of sweat covered his face. His breathing had become shallow.

"Brewster?" Noonan prompted him. Brewster just stared vaguely back at him, his eyes registering nothing. He shook him. "Can you hear me? Brewster, stay with me!"

Just then, the sound of the Mercedes' engine exploded through the car park, the sudden loud sound bouncing off the walls. Katharina was twisted round in the driver's seat, hurriedly beckoning them in.

"Right, this is it," Noonan whispered to Brewster, picking him up and half-carrying, half-dragging his body towards the car. He opened the left-hand back door and carefully shovelled Brewster's body across the black leather seat. He placed the safety deposit box on the floor behind the passenger seat. Then he went round to the opposite door and climbed in, resting Brewster's head on his knees. He looked up at Katharina, catching her eyes in the rear-view mirror.

"Go!" he ordered her. Katharina eyes briefly blazed with fury. Then a second later she had thrown the Mercedes into first gear and was gunning the engine. The Mercedes edged its way gently through the underground car park, up the ramp and into the street.

"Gently now," Noonan advised, his jaw clenched.

239

"Look, either let me drive this thing or get out now!" Katharina shot back, her tense, angry eyes catching Noonan's in the rear-view mirror again. At that moment, Brewster started moaning loudly in agony.

"Can't you shut him up, for God's sake?" Katharina yelled, her voice cracking with emotion. Noonan was too preoccupied with Brewster to reply. The side of his outfit was caked in black, dry blood and his face had assumed a white, ghostly pallor. His eyes looked up desperately at Noonan. His mouth moved as if trying to share something of great importance, but no words came out. Noonan tried to reassure him with his eyes. He had no words either, just the determination to keep him alive at all costs and not let him fall into the hands of the police. He had given Brewster his word about that. He was a marked man and being captured by the police would be tantamount to a death sentence. He was more determined than ever to avoid capture by Spender and keep all three of them free. He now had the box, which for the first time gave him the advantage over Spender and Lomax. If they got out of this mess, he would set up meeting with

Spender to exchange the box for Anna.
Katharina was keeping the Mercedes
cruising gently along at thirty miles per
hour.

"So far, so good," Noonan
murmured, more to himself than anything
else. It was too good to last. From two
side streets the horribly familiar shape of
two pale blue police cars swept out onto the
main road and roared up behind them. A
second later the night was filled with the
sickening, ear-splitting shriek of the two-
tone police sirens that screamed through
the night.

"Shit!" barked Katharina,
slamming the steering wheel with the flat
palm of her hand.

"Right, go! Go!" Noonan yelled.
But Katharina's instincts had already
kicked in and Noonan felt the pit of his
stomach drop away as the car shot forward
at terrifying speed. Noonan looked behind
him and the police car was already
dropping away into the distance. Very
quickly it accelerated fast to close the gap.
Katharina's driving skills were such that it
struggled to gain on them. Noonan
glanced quickly at his watch: 11.30.

Traffic would be at its lightest; just taxis, lorries and the occasional late-night partygoer would be out now. This was the only advantage they had. Noonan's heart sank further when he saw in the distance multiple blue lights blazing through the darkness like a light show. He had been ready for something like this; he had known that Spender would have surrounded the whole area with Metropolitan police drivers. He had effectively thrown a net over the whole area. Noonan could see no alternative.

"Go through them!" Noonan instructed her urgently.

"Shut up!" Katharina snapped. She was already doing it. Noonan felt icicles of fear creep down his back as Katharina pressed down hard on the accelerator. Under her breath she muttered a quiet *"Scheissen"*, as though it were a quiet prayer. Noonan already felt his head beginning to spin as he anticipated the sickening crunch and squeal of metal on metal, the horrifying jolt as the vehicles collided. Noonan held Brewster's body tightly to him as the gathering of police cars ahead got closer. Three seconds... Two... One... Noonan leaned forward, pressing his head between the two front seats, squeezing Brewster tighter still, and forced his eyes closed, pressing them down.

BOOM!!

The sound exploded through the car with the ferocity of shotgun blast. For a second the Mercedes shuddered and rocked as the obstructing vehicles worked to bring it to a standstill. Yet somehow Katharina managed to keep it going. Noonan kept his eyes screwed shut, not daring to open them. He ground his teeth together. He heard – or thought he heard – the sound of Brewster crying out over the screeching of shattering glass and twisting metal. Then, miraculously, he felt the Mercedes accelerating away again. He muttered "Thank you" under his breath. Then he slowly opened his eyes again. The road ahead was clear. A white car appeared round the corner and quickly mounted the pavement as Katharina came tearing towards it. He turned back. The blue lights were receding quickly into the distance and Noonan could see that Katharina had torn a huge hole through the cordon. Two of the central white Rovers had had their bonnets smashed

243

away to the point that they were no longer recognisable as bonnets. One uniformed officer was on his back on the tarmac, rocking back and forth, both arms clasping at his knee, his face pointing to the sky, his mouth open in silent agony. Several officers were crowding around him, some kneeling. The two pursuing police cars had worked their way through the messy cordon and were accelerating after them again. And what of their vehicle? With it now underperforming, the two pursuing cars would have the advantage and they would be on their radios reporting their position. Noonan turned his attention to Brewster.

"Brewster…" He shook him again. "Brewster!" Brewster's eyes opened and he grimaced up at him. "Tell me about your girl, Brewster. What was her name?"

"Sheil…" Brewster started, choking back the blood. "Jean…" He gulped and seized Noonan's shoulder. "I'm going to get that bastard Caldwell. "I'm going to…"

"I know you will, Brewster," The words shot out of him like bullets from a machine gun. "But tell me more about

Jean. What was she like? Was she tall? Blond?" He lifted Brewster's head, forcing him to look into his eyes. "Talk to me, John!

Brewster opened his mouth, but only a gasp of pain came out. His eyes started to dull over. He was losing him again.

"I'm going to look at your wound," Noonan told him urgently. He tried to lift Brewster's arms in the cramped space of the back seat, uncomfortably managing to loosen his rucksack and pull it from his shoulders. He turned Brewster over, lifted his hand and checked for a pulse, which beat slowly. His face was almost white now. Suddenly Noonan was thrown backwards hard against the door as Katharina screamed around a corner like a car at a funfair. Noonan hurriedly recovered his position and unfastened Brewster's black overalls, ripping the two sides away. He examined his chest, which was now covered in charred, dry blood. He tapped around with his fingers and located the wound to the side of the chest, which was pumping out fresh blood. He then ran his fingers around Brewster's back but found no exit wound.

"John, can you hear me?" Noonan put his ear to Brewster's mouth. No sound came out, but he nodded. "The bullet is still stuck in there. I've got to try and remove it. Now where's that knife?" Before Brewster could attempt a reply, Noonan was already searching his body and found it tucked into his boot. He pulled it out and wiped it thoroughly on the arm of his overalls. He looked at Brewster and smiled grimly. "I don't want to get any of Lomax's blood mixed up with yours... Hold tight now..."

He pulled Brewster's overalls taut and tore several large strips out of it. He then slashed around the material that made up the right arm, which came quickly away. He slipped the knife into the entry wound. Brewster began thrashing around in agony as the knife lanced into his flesh. Noonan tried to hold the knife steady, but it was impossible in the back of the car as he was thrown about. The knife tore away at Brewster's skin, causing Brewster to cry out in agony. He gripped Noonan's wrist fiercely. Blood began to explode out of the now-gaping wound. Noonan went inside the wound with his knife and prodded about.

Brewster's expression turned into a frightful grimace and a horrible guttural sound exploded from his mouth. After a few agonising seconds, Noonan pulled the knife out and gave him a terrible look. Brewster's eyes shone with awful desperation.

"The bullet's lodged tight in there, John. I can't get it out. If I try, it will kill you. I'll have to leave it in." Brewster simply nodded, his eyes sanguine and accepting. He reached weakly up and took Noonan's arm. Then his eyes closed, and his head fell back. Noonan checked his pulse again; he was still breathing. Noonan hurriedly stuffed the material from the overalls into two large balls to block the entry wound, then wrapped the arm around Brewster's body, tying it tight to make a temporary bandage. It would have to do. He laid Brewster back across his knee and turned his attention back to the road ahead.

Noonan could hear a new growling sound coming from the engine as it protested furiously. There was also a harsh scraping sound coming from the bonnet. The bodywork on the left-hand front corner had been knocked out of shape and was being dragged along the road. He could hear that part of the suspension had become destabilised. A spider's web had spread across the front windscreen and Katharina was peering intensely through it to see the way ahead. She kept the car tearing along the main road at around sixty miles per hour, a terrifying speed in the centre of London. The familiar black hulk of a London taxi swept out suddenly from a street on the right. Instantly it braked to avoid colliding with them and Katharina had to tear into a lit up sleeping policeman to avoid it. The taxi's horn honked in fury after them. Noonan turned again; the two police cars had dropped back a little but were keeping them in plain sight, which meant that the reinforcements would be on them soon. Noonan glanced up and caught Katharina's hardened, determined eyes in the rear-view mirror. She drove fearlessly and, he had to admit, beautifully. She was completely in control.

Up ahead the sound of sirens began to intensify and, as they passed signs pointing the way towards Shepherds Bush, police vehicles began to spill out from every side street. One pulled up alongside

Katharina on the right. Coolly she twisted the wheel hard and smashed the Mercedes into the side of the police car. There was a loud crack, and the police car mounted the pavement, crashing into the masonry of a shopfront. Two more police cars screamed towards them, willing them to stop. Katharina did not back down, however, and accelerated aggressively into the oncoming vehicles. Noonan again found himself involuntarily screwing his eyes tight shut again. But the collision he was anticipating never came. Instead, there came a teeth-shattering crunch from behind. Noonan snapped his head round and one of the oncoming police cars had crashed straight into one of the pursuing police cars. Both cars had become fused together in an unwieldy marriage of twisted metal and smashed glass. The impact of the collision had forced one of the cars up onto the pavement. The other police car had simply swept out of Katharina's way and had braked to a halt at a forty-five-degree angle. Its driver was stumbling out, his young, scared face lit by the flashing blue lights.

They roared past Holland Park on the right and at a roundabout ahead,

Katharina took the car up the Westway towards North Acton. Still the police cars kept coming after them, more and more of them, multiplying like locusts. Brewster was crying out in pain again but at least Noonan could feel no more fresh blood seeping out onto his fingertips. His mind was working feverishly to figure a way out of this mess. There was no way they could out-run the mobile units; there were too many of them and they would get them eventually, despite Katharina's undeniable prowess.

Disaster had been pending from the moment they had started their getaway and now, finally, it had come round to collect. Katharina took a sharp corner into North Acton at close to seventy miles an hour and suddenly an enormous lorry was in front of them, driving at half their speed, seemingly taking up the whole road. There was no time. Katharina immediately slammed her foot on the brakes, but a collision was inevitable. Katharina forced the wheel to the left, sending the car spinning in the road. The rear right hand corner of the car took the impact of the hit. The vehicle slammed to a complete halt and for a few seconds there was a terrible silence. Noonan was shaken out of his state of near total shock by the sound of the approaching, wailing sirens. Katharina had already kicked her door open and was squeezing her body through the gap between the back of the lorry and the Mercedes. The right-hand door was up against the back of the lorry, sealing him in. Instantly Noonan kicked the left-hand door open and hurled himself out into the night. He turned and hauled Brewster out of the car.

"I can move," Brewster said in a muffled voice. Noonan reached in and picked up the safety deposit box with his other hand. The police cars were now screaming down the street towards them, their headlights catching them in their glare.

"This way!" Katharina was beckoning them desperately towards a thin alleyway completely shrouded in darkness. Noonan led Brewster with his arm towards it, but Brewster was able to move on his own. They followed Katharina into the darkness and felt their way through. The alleyway was about one hundred metres in length, and it emerged onto another main road. Noonan looked around desperately.

A railway line ran parallel to the main road, and he could see in the shadows an iron bridge stretching up into the black night. Behind him, the alley was lit blue by the blazing police cars. He could hear muffled voices and running feet several feet behind him.

"The bridge!" he barked urgently. The three of them ran across the road. Noonan was vaguely aware of a van turning a corner and catching them in its headlights. They made it to the other side of the road and began to run up the steps and over the bridge.

19

Katharina ran ahead as Noonan helped Brewster over the bridge. He could feel Brewster's body sagging more and more and he was having to work harder to keep him upright. Without Noonan's support, Brewster would be in danger of toppling over and not having the strength to get back up again. He was moaning loudly in pain. Noonan knew his time was running out fast but blocked this from his mind.

The night was filled with the piercing shrieks of police sirens behind and ahead of them. There would be more police to deal with on the other side. Up ahead Katharina turned and disappeared through a gap in the fence. Noonan helped Brewster through the hole and followed. He found himself sliding down a slippery grass embankment. He dropped to his backside, pulling Brewster down with him, and they both slid down the slope together. For a brief instant Noonan was reminded of one winter he spent tobogganing with a group of friends. But then his feet hit the shingle at the bottom, and he was aware of Katharina standing over him. He pulled Brewster to his feet and looked around.

They were on a wide expanse of railway tracks, many criss-crossing each other. The darkness of the night was blasted by the occasional disruption of blue police lights exploding from the roads on either side. Katharina took Brewster's other arm, and they helped him across the messy tangle of tracks. From the right came the steady chug and clatter of a locomotive moving towards them. An engine that had been carrying cars of coal was heading determinedly towards them at low speed. A container came up alongside them. Katharina nodded to Noonan and made a grab for the ladder. Her fingers grasped the iron rung and she swung onto it. Noonan lifted Brewster's body and Katharina took him with her other hand. Noonan was now running alongside the train. Katharina climbed to the top of the container and sat on the tarpaulin covering the coal. Brewster managed to slowly climb up the ladder, Katharina pulling him. At the top he collapsed and lay on his stomach, his legs hanging over the side. The locomotive gathered speed and Noonan was forced to run harder, gripping the deposit box desperately with his left hand while reaching wildly out with his right to grab on to the steel rungs of the ladder. He made a desperate lunge for it. His hand caught the rung, he lifted off with his feet, and his body was suddenly swinging in the air, rocketed, and buffeted about by the speed of the locomotive. His other hand clung fiercely to the box. With great effort, he lifted this towards Katharina, who took it from him. His feet found the bottom rung and frantically he climbed up the ladder. At the top he moved Brewster's legs so that he was firmly on the tarpaulin.

The locomotive clattered on into the night with the strict rhythm of a metronome. The horribly familiar rumble of a helicopter thundered in the distance. Katharina heard it too and dived for the tarpaulin. She unhooked one of the bindings on the side and pulled it back to reveal a black void. She jumped into this, her lithe body disappearing under the tarpaulin. Noonan then helped Brewster underneath it and climbed in after him.

The container smelled of coal but was empty. The coal coming down from the north had presumably been recently unloaded, yet the smell of it hung heavily in the air, getting inside their lungs. Their bodies dropped four feet to the floor and fell backwards against the sides. Noonan quickly scanned the skies and saw a distant pinprick of light to the left puncturing the black sky. He quickly stood up, pulled the tarpaulin back into place and hooked the binding up again. It was pitch black under there and the air was stuffy. Noonan rolled back, his body hitting the side of the car again. A second later he felt Katharina's body tumbling against his and pressing hard against it. The thunder of the helicopter increased until Noonan could see the top of the tarpaulin caught in the glare of the searchlight. For a second the space around them was lit in a sickly green glow, long enough for Noonan to see that Brewster's body had slid to the other side of the container. Then they were plunged into blackness again. The helicopter appeared to be hovering over them for what seemed like a whole minute. Despite the chilliness of the night, Noonan could feel sweat running down his back. His mind screamed at the helicopter, willing it to disappear.

The intensity of the rumble in his ears eventually began to subside. Soon it was just a distant growl in the sky, though it was impossible to tell which direction it was heading in. Then the sound was replaced by the familiar clatter of the train wheels. Noonan closed his eyes for a second. What a mess! Spender was tearing the city apart in his efforts to find them. The police cars and helicopters would be out all night. Noonan resigned himself to the fact that they were going to be stuck inside this black, filthy hole for the next few hours. The walls and floor of the container were covered with the black, filthy residue of coal. With any luck they would be out of the metropolis by morning. And what of Lomax? They had left him in the bank vault, with a knife injury to the ankle. But Noonan sincerely doubted that that would slow him down or that the police would have him. Lomax would be out there right now, sweeping through the night like a ghost, searching for them alone. Despite the enormous manpower that Spender had at his disposal, Noonan was much more afraid of Lomax. The most pressing issue for the moment, however, was Brewster. Noonan had to do all he could for him in the time he had left. He scrambled clumsily around to the other side, where Brewster was sprawled against the corner. Noonan turned him round and tried to lift him comfortably into a sitting position, Brewster all the while growling out in pain. His breath came out slowly. Noonan was then aware of Katharina scrambling towards them from the left. She kneeled next to Brewster.

"He's dying," Noonan told her simply.

"You did all you could," she reassured him in a soft voice.

Suddenly Noonan felt a surge of anger ripping through him. He lifted his arm and furiously punched the side of the container in front of him. He immediately felt Katharina's hand slapping down on his arm. "Stop it!" she ordered, her voice hard and Germanic. She was looking at him fiercely. Then she said in a quieter voice, "We must think of ourselves now. We're not out of this yet." Noonan fell back to the floor, the roughness of the residue pressing into his back. He gently shifted

258

himself into a corner of the car. Katharina, watching him carefully, slid over and positioned herself next to him. She did not move, but Noonan was glad to be feeling the warmth of her body next to his.   He reached forward for the safety deposit box and wrapped it tightly in his arms, as though terrified it would be forced away from him.   He tried to empty his mind of all thoughts.   His head gently fell against Katharina's, and she took his hand.   Soon the waves of sleepiness were floating over him again and he felt his eyes closing.   A fitful sleep gently took him away from it all for a while...

        Noonan awoke with a start a few hours later.   He shook his head, dispelling all feelings of drowsiness and looked around.   Early daylight was now filtering through the gaps between the tarpaulin and the sides of the car.   His arms still clasped the box. He estimated that it must be about seven o'clock in the morning and that he must have slept on and off for around six hours. His first thought was of Brewster. He snapped himself into action and slid over to his body.   He checked his pulse and felt what he expected: nothing;

there was no longer any life there. He numbed himself to the fact.

Katharina's voice came from the side. She had moved since he had fallen asleep. He could see her face now with the approach of morning, blackened with coal dust. "He's been dead for at least an hour," she told him, her voice strained and fatigued. "It's just us now."

PART III

<u>20</u>

Noonan and Katharina could feel the locomotive grinding to a halt and stopping. They carefully poked their heads out. Cornfields stretched out all around, the stalks rising hopefully and hopelessly to the sky. The sky was a deep, azure blue and it was the start of a beautiful late winter's day. The sun was strong and low in the sky, hitting Noonan's face with warmth as he smelled the countryside all around. There was no sign of any civilisation. Finally, the locomotive stopped with a final jolt. Noonan leaned further out and saw that the train was being held at a red light. He looked at Katharina and they nodded, reading each other's thoughts. It was time to get out. Noonan moved to Brewster's body and quickly ran his hands up and down his front and back. He found what he was looking for in the right hand back trouser pocket. He pulled the passports out and, unseen by Katharina, quickly hid them in his pocket.

"What are you doing?" she suddenly wanted to know, her voice loaded with suspicion.

"Seeing what he's got on him." He turned back to her. "Nothing."

"What do we do with him?"

"Leave him here. There's nothing more we can do."

Noonan carefully positioned Brewster's body into a sitting position in the corner of the car and closed his eyes. He squeezed his shoulder tenderly once. Katharina was already squeezing herself out through the tarpaulin. He shifted to the side, carefully peeled it away and fed his legs through the gap. He came out backwards, his feet finding the rungs of the ladder. To his right, Katharina jumped to the ground. In his right hand he gripped the safety deposit box. He worked his way down the ladder, turned and stepped carefully over the rails. There was a patch of long grass by the side of the railway. Katharina and Noonan ran for its cover, crouching down. They stayed like that for five minutes before the locomotive let out a long, slow sigh and began to wheeze back into action. The various cars clanked and chattered away to each other as the locomotive went on its way. Soon the last car passed them, and the great beast was disappearing up the line. It growled into the distance, and all was suddenly quiet and still. Noonan watched it disappear.

"I'm sorry, Brewster," he muttered quietly, almost to himself. Then he looked all around. "Where the hell are we?" he mused to himself. From the look of the countryside, he decided it had to Hertfordshire. "Come on, let's walk." He picked up the box and stepped carefully back across the railway line.

There was a long track separating two cornfields and this looked the best way forward. Noonan was halfway over the tracks when a sudden thought struck him. His hand dropped to his belt for the butt of the gun. It was not there. A second later he heard a familiar metallic click. He stopped in his tracks just as he was at the foot of the path. He turned slowly.

Katharina was standing on the other side of the railway line, the Browning .9mm pointing straight at him.

"You're a fool, Noonan. You were so concerned about Brewster that you forgot about me."

Noonan looked beyond the gun that the girl was holding levelly in front of her and into her cool, confident eyes. "If you're going to shoot, Katharina, you'd better do it now. You won't get another chance like this." He paused. "You'd probably be doing me a favour in any case."

Katharina did not immediately reply. Noonan suddenly felt a cool gust of wind blowing across his face and a bird chirruped somewhere off to the side. It was a peaceful, bucolic scene. Noonan decided it did not matter what happened now. There seemed to be no way out of this endless cycle of violence that he found himself caught up in. He had failed to save both Anna and now Brewster. He had become thoroughly worn down by the likes of Spender and Lomax. At least he would finally be away from them. Finally, Katharina spoke again.

"I'm out now," she said. "This isn't my fight."

"Alright, you're out," Noonan replied. "That's fine. But how far do you think you'll get?"

"I've survived on my own."

Noonan shook his head. "It's different this time."

A moment of doubt passed across her eyes. "How?"

"Because this time you're up against Lomax. You asked me once what he had over me."

"Well?"

"A girl called Anna. He's holding her somewhere." The gun did not waver. "I made a deal with a man called Spender. I was going to deliver Lomax to him in return for Anna."

"What does this have to do with me?"

Noonan raised the safety deposit box in his right hand slightly. "This is Lomax's own safety deposit box. Inside it is every dirty secret you could possibly

267

imagine. He was going to skip the country with it."

"How does it help me?"

"For as long as we've got it, we're in control. It's the one thing that guarantees our safety. Lomax and Spender will do anything to get their hands on it." Noonan paused. He could see her eyes beginning to soften as she understood. "So, you see; if you try to get away on your own, you'll be in a German prison before the week's out. This way at least you have a chance."

"Why don't I just kill you now and take the box?"

"Because you won't make it on your own. Like it or not, we need each other."

She searched his face for the truth behind his words. Then gently, she eased the hammer back into position but kept the gun pointing at him. "So, what have you got in mind?"

"We'll be front page news by now," Noonan replied, looking carefully at her. "Spender will have every police force in the country out looking for us. If they don't already have our names and photographs, then they will soon. So, we'll have to find a place to lay low for a while. We also need to get this box open. We should then be able to find Lomax's home ground. We can lay a trap for him there, using Spender. Spender then gets Lomax, and we get Spender to agree to our demands."

"You've got it all worked out, haven't you?" Katharina looked at him for a long moment. "Alright," she finally said, letting the gun fall to her side and stuffing it into the pocket of her overalls.

Noonan turned away from her with weary resignation and self-disgust. He started walking away. Everything he had just told her was true, but he wanted to be away from her, away from everyone and everything. He had become sickened by the whole business. It was a beautiful morning and the air smelt fresh. He may as well enjoy it and forget all about the other business. He could not remember the last time he had enjoyed a good walk in the country. Probably not since North Devon when he had first encountered Anna. He inhaled the crisp morning air into his lungs and felt good. The safety deposit box banged relentlessly against his right ankle.

Suddenly he could hear footsteps next to his and his mood suddenly dampened. He turned and saw Katharina walking briskly alongside him. She was not looking at him. They walked like this in silence for two hours, the track stretching out in front of them, drawing them in through the miles of corn. Noonan estimated that they must have walked about five miles. All the time, he was feeling an increasing sense of dread, unease and foreboding as the walk continued. He was feeling more and more exposed out here in the empty countryside. He continually looked around and to his back, across the wide oceans of corn, half expecting to see Lomax suddenly appearing out of nowhere. He was certainly feeling him out there in the wilderness, getting closer all the time. The track dipped down into a valley with a farmhouse at the bottom. At this point, they reached a crossroads and the cornfields stopped here. The track continued upwards through a barren patch.

"Which way?" Katharina asked.

Noonan pointed to the path going left. "This way?"

"Yes, I think so," Katharina nodded.

The path was thinner and framed by two hedgerows. They met their first stranger along it, an elderly gentleman in a cloth cap with a Labrador who looked like a retired QC. Noonan considered their blackened faces and dishevelled appearances and lowered his face. He wondered how they would appear to him. He found out quickly enough. The gentleman glanced at them both for a second then cast his eyes down again. As he passed, he said in a refined voice, "You look like you've been in the wars." He walked by without further comment and was gone. Noonan laughed then and could not remember the last time he had. He turned to Katharina who was looking blankly at him. He shook his head at her and started walking again.

The countryside around them became greener and lusher as they progressed along the path. They were now surrounded by meadows of long grass and cattle. They eventually reached a narrow country line. The path continued the other side but became progressively narrower. They saw no-one. In the distance, Noonan glimpsed the chimney of what looked like a farm building jutting upwards from a valley about half a mile away. He turned to Katharina. "When we get to that farm, we need to get that box open," he told her. "Can you blow it?"

"I can blow it," she replied, "but there's bound to be superficial damage to the items."

Noonan shrugged. "Risk we have to take."

"Noonan..." Katharina began. He turned to her. "The police will have Lomax by now. Won't they?"

"No. He'll be coming after us right now."

"How do you know?"

Noonan just looked at her once. "I know."

"Jesus," Katharina whistled grimly. "You're really frightened of him, aren't you?"

Noonan did not answer, just walked on slightly ahead. Katharina's question had dampened both their spirits. They trudged on in weary silence over the brow of the hill. At the top, they could see the farm building nestling in the bottom of the valley. An empty, adjacent barn stood next to it. Noonan scanned the surrounding area. Only a dilapidated tractor stood in the front courtyard, surrounded by empty, brown fields. The place appeared to be empty. Katharina turned to him and nodded. They jogged quickly down the track and crouched down behind the tractor, their breath coming out hard and fast. Katharina looked over the farm building.

"What do you think?"

Before Noonan could reply, the distant rumble of an approaching vehicle filled the air from the other side of the hill. "Move!" he hissed. They sprinted into the barn, Katharina hurling herself through the door before the vehicle appeared over the top of the hill. Noonan crouched down, peering through a gap between two slats. A red van was moving towards the farm building, throwing up a trail of dust in its wake. Noonan saw a logo on the side and was quickly able to discern that this was a Royal Mail van. It growled to a halt. The door opened and a young man with long hair hanging round his ears stepped out, carrying some letters in one hand and a newspaper in the other. Glancing disinterestedly around the building, he walked up to the front door. He shoved the letters through the letterbox but left the newspaper stuck in it. Then, his duty discharged, he marched quickly back to his van, got in, started the engine, performed a three-point turn in the drive, and punched the van back up the hill. Noonan watched it disappear over the rim. Once the distant rumble had subsided, he and Katharina stayed frozen in their positions, their eyes pinned to the front of the farmhouse. Noonan watched the newspaper in the letterbox, but it never moved. He glanced carefully along all the windows, seeing nothing. He looked then at Katharina, and she nodded. They stood up and moved carefully back into the courtyard. Noonan darted to the front door, watching all the windows carefully as he did so. He ripped the newspaper out of the letter box and unfolded it. Katharina joined him. They both looked at the front page. Across it were three black and white photographs. Noonan did not have to look long to recognise the images of Brewster, Spanton and Katharina staring back at him. The bold print, splashed across the top read: "ONE KILLED AND TWO SOUGHT IN VIOLENT ROBBERY". He shuddered involuntarily. He had suspected it, but now it was official: they were front page news and every police constabulary in the country would now be looking for them.

21

Noonan looked down at the body of the text, his eyes hurriedly scanning the contents. He read the following:

"One of the fugitives has been positively identified as Katharina Vogel, former member of the Richter-Hoffman terrorist cell, and the only member still at large. She has been on the missing list for six months, following the arrest and prosecution of the rest of the gang in Hamburg, Germany. Scotland Yard have issued a statement warning all members of the public not to approach if sighted, but to telephone the police immediately..."

He did not read about Brewster. Whatever they had written could no longer hurt him. In one corner of the front page was the increasingly familiar face of Dr Julius Obana, the African diplomat who had recently disappeared and Scotland Yard were still searching for. How had they managed to become front page news so quickly? The job had only ended a few hours ago. There was only one conclusion: Spender must have used his influence to get the story to run just in case anything went wrong. Spender left nothing to chance, but neither did Lomax, who had no idea where to look right now, but would be monitoring the police radio traffic for any sightings. They would just have to remain hidden.

"Nothing about you?" Katharina's voice was slippery with suspicion. Noonan did not reply, just stuffed the newspaper back into the letterbox. Katharina started walking round the side of the farmhouse. A steep hill full of corn rose around the back. Noonan quickly followed her. Katharina ducked her head whenever she came to a window and disappeared round the back. Noonan joined her seconds later, where he found her waiting by a sturdy back door. She carefully gripped the black handle and pressed down. The door was locked. She took a handkerchief out of the overall pocket and wrapped it around her fist. With her other hand she pulled out the gun and held the butt up to the glass pane. She brought her arm back and smashed it out. She carefully reached in and unlocked the door. She pushed it gently inwards and stepped inside, delicately stepping over the fragments of glass that lay scattered across the brown doormat. Noonan followed her lead, closing the door behind him.

The farmhouse was made of solid oak and smelled musty, as though the windows had not been opened for a few days. The corridor led to a door which led into a small but cosy drawing room. The door beyond it led to a reception area and, off to the left, a small kitchen with red tiles on the floor and a wooden table in the centre. As Noonan moved silently through the house, his ears tuned to detect the slightest sound. He looked out of the window, checking the drive, and set the deposit box down. He sat at the table, facing the window so that he could see any activity outside. Katharina remained standing, pacing awkwardly and impatiently, the gun still in her hand.

"The box," Noonan nodded to her. Katharina opened her rucksack and carefully removed a small amount of

Semtex. "How much of that stuff do you need?"

"Tiny amount," she replied in a quiet voice. She carefully moved the box to the edge of the table and knelt on the cold floor. She drove a tiny ball of the Semtex into the lock and unwound the coil of fuse. She turned to Noonan. "Get back," she ordered him. Noonan promptly took a couple of steps back. "Right back!" she reiterated in a harder voice. "Against the door!" Noonan did not argue, moving quickly to the door and crouching down. Katharina took out the lighter and lit the end of the fuse, which sparkled and crackled. She dived backwards and nestled herself into Noonan's body. He pressed his face into the back of her neck, closing his eyes, bracing himself. There was a loud 'pop'. Noonan looked up. A cloud of black smoke was rising to the ceiling. The minor explosion had left an angry, black scorch mark across the table. The lock had exploded outwards, leaving a jagged hole and a dent in its place. Noonan stood up, moving towards the box.

"Careful!" Katharina ordered him. Noonan reached into his pocket and took out a glove for his right hand. He put it on and carefully lifted the lid of the box. He waved the last of the smoke away. Inside was a deep pile of papers and documents. Noonan lifted these out and placed them on the table. He lifted the pages at the top. The bottom edges had been caught by Katharina's Semtex, leaving them with an inch of crisp, brown damage. The pungent smell of burning filled the air. The content of the material however was mercifully intact.

Noonan turned to Katharina. "Thank you," he said to her quietly. She came forward from the door, her eyes sparkling with curiosity, even fear. Noonan pulled a chair out, sat down and picked up the first pile. Katharina gave the papers a cursory glance and then quickly moved away. Noonan started running his eyes over the papers; the papers that certain men would kill for; the papers that had caused so much pain and misery and had meant the death of many already. But Noonan was only interested in one piece of information, one piece of a jigsaw puzzle among thousands. He skipped through the priceless pieces of information as though they were headlines from last year's newspapers. Lists of agents operating overseas and their cover names; top secret government installations working on the illegal testing of chemical nerve gases that could be used in military conflicts; various members of Parliament, some of whom Noonan recognised as being very much in the public eye, caught on camera *in flagrante delicto* for the purposes of blackmail; other various indiscretions and acts of treachery, logged, monitored, and recorded. Noonan felt as though his fingers were being dirtied at the touch of every filthy sheet. Lomax seemingly had gathered destructive dirt on everyone who mattered. He found documents that approved the British financing of mercenary invasions into politically corrupt African states. Spender's name was all over those documents. No wonder he was so keen to get his hands on this stuff.

Behind him, Noonan heard Katharina exhaling nervously and impatiently. He looked behind him. She had positioned herself behind the wall and was carefully watching the outside. She turned and looked at him, her eyes flashing with urgency.

"How much longer?"

"As long as it takes."

"Christ," she muttered under her breath, before turning back to the window. Noonan got back to the papers. After several minutes Noonan was feeling queasy. If there had been any vestiges of doubt left in his mind that the world was, at its heart, rotten to the core, then this box had remorselessly stamped them out.

Three quarters of the way down, Noonan came to a separate, navy-blue file made of card. Unthinkingly, he tore the file out of the box. Inside were a series of black and white photographs of what appeared to be ordinary people, photographed surreptitiously, mostly young women. Noonan flipped the photographs over. The names and addresses of each person had been neatly written in black biro on the back of each, along with a date, the earliest dating back to 1967. The earliest photograph belonged to one Beatrice Tanner, the young wife of Derek Tanner, a naval officer with a promising career ahead of him, who had committed suicide in mysterious circumstances. Beatrice had seemingly vanished without trace the following week, never to be seen again. Noonan vaguely remembered it being in the news at the time.　He felt a rush of excitement.　He felt Anna getting closer all the time.

He gave the rest of the photographs a cursory glance, recognising some of the names from the headlines without being immediately able to recall the details. The final photograph was dated September 1971.　One feature that the final five photographs all had in common was the words "Oldershaw Manor Park" written in neat red lettering on the back.　Oldershaw Manor Park?　The name seemed to ring a distant bell in his memory.　Yes! Gloucestershire!　Lomax had taken him there once but had made him wait for him in the car.　Lomax had been particular about not wanting him to see inside the place.　It was a huge, opulent estate in the Gloucestershire countryside, which he was certain Lomax owned.　But would he ever be able to find it again?　If only there was an address to go with it!

The next item was another navy-blue file.　Stamped across this one was his own name in thick, black, bold lettering. Noonan could not imagine that he could feel any sicker than he already did, but the waves of nausea intensified still.　He angrily ripped out the black and white photographs. The first was a shot of himself and Anna outside their Cotswolds cottage, leaning into each other and smiling. He felt his blood draining from his face. He flipped the photograph over. The date 13/12/1972 had been scrawled on the back in black felt tip. He thumbed quickly through the other photographs, which went backwards in time. The next photographs he recognised as having been taken in Denby, the village in which he had first met Anna. The top one was a shot of them walking together at dusk. He remembered that evening well; it was the first time he had met her, and he had walked her home. He flipped the photograph over. The date 06/10/1972 had been scrawled on the back. Noonan could not bring himself to look at the other photographs. He shoved them back in the file and slammed it back into the box. So, Lomax had been onto him all along! The vicious, cunning, ruthless bastard...

He took a few seconds to clear his head then continued with his work. The only other item in the box that interested him came right at the end. It was a portfolio of a development in Maui, Hawaii called Kahiau. Noonan glanced through this, finding architects plans and photographs of the development in various stages of construction. So, this was Lomax's retirement plan! Once again, he committed the name firmly into the memory banks of his mind. He sat there, working the information over in his mind, thinking, planning, hoping...

He was snapped out of his thoughts by Katharina's voice. "Well?"

"I think the answer is in Gloucestershire," he replied, his tone brisk and business-like. "It's a large country estate, Oldershaw Manor Park. Lomax took me there once. That's where we need to go."

"On foot?" She glowered impatiently at him.

"No, I don't think we'll need to," he replied, leaning back slightly. He found himself remembering her wonderful performance in the car the previous evening. "You drove magnificently last night," he said to her. "We never would have got out of that place without you."

"You did alright yourself," she replied simply with a shrug. "What about your girl?

"I think she's there. It's a place where people disappear." He looked back at the papers spread out across the kitchen table. "I wonder if there's a suitcase around here," he mused. He stood up quickly and left the room. Katharina followed him out into the hallway. He tried a door to the left, which opened into a small study. A beige packing case was sitting on top of a pile of boxes. Noonan reached up and lifted it down. Katharina stood leaning up against the door, watching him impatiently. He opened the case, removing a pile of wooden frames inside and placing them down on a study desk. Noonan and Katharina moved swiftly back into the kitchen.

At that moment, Noonan was suddenly jolted by the sound of a vehicle swooshing into the drive, the crunch of tyres on gravel and the grinding of brakes. He swore under his breath and clumsily whipped up all the sheets of paper, thrusting them back into the deposit box, which he then slammed into the suitcase,

286

snapping the two locks shut. Katharina was pulling the gun out of her overalls.

"Move!" she hissed. Noonan heard the dull boom of car doors being shut and footsteps walking up to the door. He was already running out of the kitchen, Katharina in front of him. They raced back down the hallway as they heard the key being inserted into the lock and turned. Katharina turned, raising the gun, ready to fire. Without thinking about it, Noonan clamped his hand down hard on the barrel of the gun, forcing it out of her hand. She hissed something in German at him but was already running. Noonan followed after her into the drawing room, closing the door behind him just as the front door opened.

Noonan and Katharina raced across the drawing room and out again through the back door. Cool air hit them and then they suddenly froze. A young girl about seven years old was standing directly in front of them, her eyes wide with terror. She was clutching a doll in one arm. She saw the gun in Noonan's hand. A second later she started screaming at the top of her voice, again and again. Noonan and Katharina raced past her, running hard for the fence at the end of the backyard. They made it there, vaulted over it, and started the long climb through the long grass to the top of the hill. Behind him he could still hear the screams of the little girl crashing into his ears. Mixed in with this were the raised voices of two adults, presumably the parents who owned the farm. The suitcase smashed viciously against his shin, weighing heavily, and slowing him down.

As they neared the top of the hill, Noonan dared to look round and saw what he suspected, feared, he would see. The distant figure of the farmer was standing in the backyard aiming a shotgun at them.

"Down!" Noonan shouted, pulling Katharina down with him. In that instant, the shotgun barked out at them from the valley below. Noonan rolled to safety in the long grass. The second round exploded across the valley a second later. Noonan calculated that it would take the farmer twenty to thirty seconds to reload. He grabbed Katharina and they raced up the last lap of the hill, disappearing over the rim just as the shotgun erupted angrily again from behind them.

Noonan saw an ocean of corn getting ready for Spring all around him. They ran through this as hard as they could. In his mind Noonan was counting off the minutes. He figured it would take a while after the farmer had inevitably telephoned the police for the local constabulary to be out in vehicles roaming the area. He cursed silently; this was bound to set them back badly. And, sure enough, minutes later, he first heard the distant scream of two-tone police sirens in the distance, getting closer. Then he heard more coming from the opposite direction.

Noonan saw a road cutting through the cornfields directly up ahead. He stopped, his breathing coming out hard. Katharina stopped with him, watching him carefully. He lifted his arm up for silence. A flash of blue in the corner of his eye made him dive to his stomach, lying prone in the grass. Katharina leapt to the ground after him. He lifted his head slightly, peering over the top of the corn. Two pale blue police cars were screaming down the road, lights flashing, towards each other. They waited until the cars had shot past and the cacophony of the sirens had subsided before they picked themselves up. Listening hard, they hurriedly walked the final one hundred yards to the long straight B-road ahead of them.

They reached the black tarmac. All was quiet now apart from a dog barking loudly from somewhere in the distance. They walked along the left-hand side of the road like two weary travellers. Behind him he heard the distant hum of a car approaching from behind. Noonan turned; it was green in colour, so not a police car. Noonan instinctively put his arm around Katharina's shoulders, and he felt her pressing up close to him. Immediately then he felt the shiver of terror running down his spine. He turned again. The car was roughly one hundred yards away and approaching fast. Noonan squinted at the black figure hunched over the steering wheel, gloved fingers intently gripping it. He could not see the face, only a black, hideous shape, but one look was all Noonan needed. Katharina had had the same thought.

"Noonan!" she screamed, genuine terror in her voice.

"MOVE!" he screamed back.   He pulled her violently across the road and together they ploughed ferociously through the corn stretching away on the other side of the road.

22

"It's Lomax!" he gasped, feeling her terror as well as his own. His feet crashed through the rough ground, the stalks tearing at him, doing their best to bar their way. So, he had been listening to the police frequency and now here he was! Behind him, he could hear the car screech to a halt. "Keep running!" A second later, two loud crashes exploded across the field and Noonan instantly dropped to the ground, taking Katharina with him. He felt the whizz of the two bullets flying over their heads less than a second later. Next to him, Katharina swore violently. "Keep down!" he hissed urgently. They tore desperately and defiantly at the corn as they hacked their way through it, doubled over. Noonan felt his head brushing insistently against the swaying corn. He felt around for Katharina's hand and seized it.

Katharina suddenly grabbed Noonan and pulled him down to the ground. He went down with her, side by side, their stomachs pressing into each other. He looked at her, feeling her stomach inhaling and exhaling, as she pursed her lips in a "shush" gesture. He felt her breath on his face and held her dark, frightened eyes with his. Noonan pulled the suitcase towards him with his right arm, hugging it, not daring to breathe. He laid it down beside him, pulling the gun from his trousers and holding it out in front of him, pointing into the corn. His finger was tight on the trigger, ready to squeeze the moment he saw a flash of Lomax. He could hear his feet brushing through the corn ahead of them and to the right. The movement was irregular, Noonan remembering that he would now be limping. He was moving closer and almost on top of them. He felt Katharina prodding him. He looked at her and she was gesturing impatiently, making a gun with her two fingers, urging him to risk a shot. Noonan shook his head impatiently. He knew that Lomax would have the drop on them and would cut them down. He could not beat Lomax at this game. To move now would be suicide. Instead, Noonan lay there waiting, praying. Katharina reached over and tried to take the gun from him, but he clamped his hand firmly down on hers. They stared at each other fiercely, their ears burning. And then the feet started to slowly move away and towards the left. Noonan and Katharina stayed in their positions for what seemed like twenty minutes, both fearing that Lomax was lulling them into a trap.

Slowly, steadily, Noonan and Katharina began to crawl in the opposite direction, the gun still in Noonan's hand. All the time, his ears were attuned to pick up any unnatural sound, such as the movement of human feet. Noonan lost all track of time as they crawled. And then his face hit wire. He looked up and a barbed wire fence was blocking their way. Beyond it was a stretch of grass and beyond that, another road. The distant hum of a car coming from the right rumbled in the distance. Noonan and Katharina looked at each other, reading each other's thoughts and nodding.

Noonan indicated, lifting the lowest line of barbed wire. Katharina crawled underneath it. It seemed to take a while and Noonan felt that the noise could be heard a mile off. Then she was clear, and she held up the wire for him. He realised then that he would need to hand her the gun and he hesitated. She understood and gently put her hand over it. There was no longer any time to doubt her, and he allowed her to take the gun from him. He pushed the suitcase through, and crawled underneath as fast as he could, as she lifted the wire. Then they picked themselves up, Noonan grabbing the suitcase, and ran as fast as they could.

They made it to the road and found themselves facing the oncoming car. Noonan's heart immediately sunk as the familiar shape of a pale blue police car steadily revealed itself.

"Keep running!" Katharina cried out. They raced for the corn on the other side of the road, but the police car was already upon them. It screeched to a fault a few feet away from them, the engine still running.

"Stop right there!" The thunderous voice was followed by a shot exploding into the sky. Noonan and Katharina froze in their tracks. Noonan half-raised his arms and slowly turned around. The driver was slowly getting out and approaching, his smoking Webley Mark IV service revolver raised. He had a black moustache and a thin, pinched face. His partner, a younger man with ginger hair and a fresh, freckled, innocent face, got out of the passenger side. He was also armed, but he was holding his pistol awkwardly and uncomfortably.

"It's them, isn't it?" he called out nervously to the older man, who was clearly the senior officer. His eyes darted nervously to the older man and back to Noonan and Katharina. His gun was waving vaguely in their direction. "I think it's them!"

"One move, you bastard, and I'll drop you," the senior officer warned Noonan tersely. "Now walk slowly towards me."

Noonan stood very still; his arms held out in front of him. He turned to Katharina, who was looking directly at him, waiting for his signal. Her hands, holding the gun, were clasped behind her back.

"And you, love!" ordered the senior officer, covering her with the Webley. "And get your hands out from behind your back. Slowly!"

"Watch it, Sarge!" shouted the younger partner, his voice now audibly shaking.

Noonan communicated silently to Katharina with his eyes, and she understood. "Not permanent!" Noonan called out to her.

"What did you say?" the senior man started. "I didn't say you could...!" That was as far as he got. The shot erupted like a crash of thunder and the bullet tore through his skull, lifting a section of his head away as it did so. Noonan and Katharina dived to the grass. The second bullet followed a second later, catching the younger officer in the chest as he spun around, his pistol pointing to the sky, and sending his body crumpling against the car. Noonan momentarily caught a glimpse of Lomax's black figure standing erect at the fence, his gun raised. Then he was crawling with Katharina towards the already-open driver's door. Katharina slid quickly into the front of the car while Noonan opened the back door and catapulted himself across the back seat with the suitcase stretched out in front of him, keeping his head down. A series of shots exploded through the windows of the police car, shattering them. With lightning precision, Katharina pressed down on the clutch with her hand and put the vehicle into gear, all the while lying across the front seats. She pressed the accelerator down with the palm of her right hand and operated the steering wheel with her left. The car roared bumpily off, Katharina driving blind. She could feel the car lurching and zigzagging drunkenly down the road, alternately hitting gravel and tarmac. A series of loud thuds slammed into the body of the car. Katharina remained across the seats, hearing the angry blast of another car horn as it narrowly missed them coming from the other direction. A second later, Katharina lifted her body onto the seat and peered over the steering wheel, keeping her head down. No further shots sounded. She glanced into the rear-view mirror but could see no-one. She floored the accelerator and straightened the car up. The car flew along the country road.

"It's clear!" she barked at Noonan. Noonan lifted himself up and looked through the two front seats. The road ahead was quiet. He quickly examined the state of the car. The windows had all been blown out and it had been severely shot up. But it was still going at least.

Five minutes down the road, Katharina stopped, and Noonan got into the passenger seat. He turned the radio on, fiddling with the dials. The muffled sound of the police frequency came over faintly. Noonan listened intently, leaning forward slightly.

"Where are we going?" Katharina shouted over the noise of the wind crashing into the car. Noonan silenced her with a look, turning the volume up. Various street names and car registration numbers hissed out at him through the speaker, but so far nothing that related to them. Noonan closed his eyes for a moment and the memory of the two policemen forced its way back into his consciousness. He was seeing the bullet hitting the police driver in the head and he instantly felt the sickness rising in him again. He saw his young partner, from the look of him a mere twenty years old, crashing backwards against the car, his young life suddenly and needlessly snuffed out. Two more dead people on his conscience. Two more innocents caught in the crossfire. Officers of the law, no less. They had been brave, honourable men, whose final misfortune had been to run into himself and Katharina Vogel, and try to bring them in. He and the girl had not killed them, but they may as well have done. It had been Lomax who had gunned them down without mercy, all for the sake of a deposit box. His final reckoning with Lomax was coming shortly; and if he managed to kill him, he would remember the two policemen as he did so. He had to hope for the best and give everything he had. He would need to; this was going to be the fight of his life.

He looked all around him, the incessant buzzing of the police radio and the emptiness of the Hertfordshire countryside making him feel intensely uneasy. Several cars zipped past. He was looking far into the distance for any signs of other police cars. Suddenly, a voice from the police radio, higher in volume than the others, boomed out at them. "All cars alert! All cars alert! London robbery suspects spotted five miles outside of Tring! Two officers down! Suspects armed! Last seen driving westwards in police vehicle along A4251! All units! Approach with caution. They are armed and dangerous!"

Noonan swore under his breath. "Lomax," he spat bitterly into the wind that rocketed in through the missing car window. Katharina pressed her foot down on the accelerator, bringing the car's speed up to sixty miles per hour. A sign flew past them proclaiming, "Welcome to Buckinghamshire", and Noonan let out a sigh of relief.

By sticking to the B roads, they were able to make it safely through Buckinghamshire and into Oxfordshire, and then from Oxfordshire into Gloucestershire. Noonan and Katharina sat in silence as they made their way towards the western counties, Noonan watchful and alert for every second of the journey, Katharina following her instincts and the road signs as she guided the vehicle towards their destination. "We're getting low on fuel," she suddenly informed him the moment they had crossed the border into Gloucestershire.

"That's all we need," Noonan replied in a raised voice over the wind. "We're close, I know we're close! Follow signs to Cirencester. It's just beyond that." They quickly came across signs leading there and she followed them. They passed through Cirencester a short while later, the needle hovering ominously over the '0' on the fuel meter.

"Take the right here!" Noonan suddenly instructed her as a narrow country lane appeared to the right of them. "It's not far now!" Katharina quickly indicated and yanked the wheel round, the car screeching across the road in front of an estate car that was coming in the opposite direction. The car blared its horn in protest. The road was narrow and twisted its way through a forested area. Soon they were coming out of the woods.

And there it was!

It was exactly as he remembered it, a golden, palatial, sprawling estate fit for a king, and perfect therefore for Lomax. Carefully tended lawns stretched away on all sides and a long grey drive rolled up to the entrance.   Noonan watched it in fascination as Katharina drove towards it. There were two stories, but the property was vast and there must have been at least twenty bedrooms in there.   White stone steps led up to a wide oak front door.   The manor house itself was on a higher point, surrounded by woodlands on all sides.   A long stretch of flat grass spread out to the left of the manor house.

Then the engine began to cough and splutter in surrender.   "Scheissen!" Katharina swore, slamming her palm on the steering wheel.   The engine cut out then   and   cruised   silently,   steadily decelerating.   Katharina pulled into the side of the road, mounting the grass.   The car glided to a halt.

"Looks like we walk from here," said Noonan.   To the right was an expansive field for corn in the summer.   To the left were the woods that they were emerging from. They stretched all the way up to the property.   It would provide adequate cover.   Noonan could feel his heart beating hard inside him. He also felt something else: he felt Anna's presence close by.   He turned to Katharina.

"Are you ready?"

She nodded. "Are you certain Lomax is going to be there?"

"He'll know that I've seen inside the box," Noonan reasoned. "And he'd know I'd come here."

Katharina closed her eyes for a second and then looked ahead of her. "Let's just get it over with," she finally sighed.

23

Noonan glanced at his watch.   It was now half past five and getting dusky. The adrenalin was pumping through his body, and he felt as alert and poised as he ever had done in his life.   It had been one hell of day, which seemed to have lasted forever; it was a long way from over yet and he was about to face the most challenging part, but his senses felt more attuned than ever.   Katharina looked back at him with the same keen anticipation in her eyes.

"We can work our way through these trees to the back of the house," Noonan suggested.   He looked up at the leafless branches, leaned into the back seat and grabbed the suitcase.   He and Katharina got out of the car and moved silently through the trees with barely the rustle of a foot on a dry leaf giving away their presence. Noonan kept his eyes to the ground, checking for wires that might trip off a burglar alarm. He spotted one thin wire cutting through the brown, dried bracken. He stopped Katharina, pointed and they both stepped carefully over it. She held up a hand and Noonan halted, taking her rucksack off and opening it. She took out a small pair of wire-cutters and delicately snipped the wire. She looked up at Noonan and nodded. Before long they were facing the back of the house. Up close it looked even more grand and opulent. There was only one light showing from one of the windows at the back of the house. Noonan looked for a blind spot which would provide an opportunity to approach the house undetected. Noonan patted Katharina on the shoulder, indicating that he had found what he was looking for. There was an alcove in the centre of the house which would provide enough cover.

Noonan measured distances. The dusk would provide extra cover. He was about to break from the trees into a run when he spotted a heavy-set figure in camouflage gear and a black woollen hat walking round the side of the building from the right. To the left, a back door opened, and another figure emerged, this one wearing a black donkey jacket. Both men, with their tough, swarthy features, looked like they had been recruited from the criminal underworld. So, that was the security! Even from a distance, their hostile, suspicious eyes glittered through the dusk. The two men nodded to each other as they passed on their circuit of the house. The moment their bodies had disappeared behind the building, Noonan nodded to Katharina, and they broke cover, running hard. Noonan kept the suitcase gripped tightly in his hand and his eyes fiercely fixed to the windows of the building, but there was no movement in any of them. The golden bricks loomed ahead of them and suddenly they were there, hurling themselves into the alcove. Noonan felt his heart racing. Now they would have to wait.

Noonan gestured to Katharina by slicing a hand across his throat and she nodded. They pressed themselves hard against the wall, hoping that the shadows would swallow them up. After a minute they heard the even, regular crunch of boots on the grass. Soon the large, looming figure of one of the men crossed in front of them. Noonan leapt out, clamping his hand over the mouth, and dragging the body into the alcove. Katharina brought her hand down hard on the side of the man's face three times, silencing him. The body stopped struggling and she forced him on to the ground. Katharina hurriedly untied the man's laces and used them to tightly tie both his hands and feet. Noonan ripped off the man's tie and used it as a gag. Seconds later the second man emerged, and Noonan and Katharina performed the same routine. He quickly searched the body and pulled out a Browning Hi-Power, checking the clip. They gently laid the two bodies next to each other. Noonan peered out of the alcove, but the lawn was empty. They rushed along to the back door, hugging the shadows as much as possible and took positions on either side of the back door. They carefully looked round. A dimly lit hallway stretched ahead of them. They communicated silently and crept into the hallway.

They followed this to a narrow flight of steps going up, ending at a door. They took these carefully and listened through the door. All was silent. Noonan turned the handle and pulled. The door croaked and wheezed. He winced and froze, listening. The silence remained. He opened the door as far as he dared, giving himself enough room to twist his body through. Katharina followed quickly behind him.

They crept along a wide, ornate corridor, painted in glittering, dazzling gold. Chandeliers hung from the ceilings and portraits from the wall. Noonan imagined the inside of Buckingham Palace would look similar. Lomax certainly knew how to live. They walked carefully through the house, their eyes checking every nook and cranny, their ears tuned for any unnatural sound. Several heavy oak doors went off from both sides of the corridor. They checked all the rooms, but they were all in darkness.

The sound of footsteps suddenly echoed along the corridor. Noonan and Katharina leapt for cover behind the oak panelling of two of the doors opposite each other. Noonan pushed the suitcase up against the door, praying that it would not be visible. The footsteps increased in volume. Noonan tensed his body, imagining the figure of the man five feet away, then four, three... The black, suited figure emerged then, walking past. Noonan pounced, bringing the butt of the gun down hard on the man's temple. Katharina leapt forward, clamping her hands around the man's mouth, muffling the groans. Noonan gently let the body drop to the floor. They pulled the body into the nearest room, a small cloak room. Noonan looked down at the suited body. He was youngish, thirty, with sandy hair. He had the appearance of an officer in a regiment who had been seduced and lured away by the promise of Lomax's money. Once again, Noonan removed his tie, stuffing it into his mouth, and tied his arms and legs with his shoelaces. Noonan and Katharina quickly left the room, snapping out the lights.

They carried on down the corridor, reaching the end. A red carpeted staircase wound downwards. Noonan crept down a few steps, Katharina behind him. He peered down and saw a wooden door at the bottom. Beyond that, a girl's voice crying out suddenly cut through the air. Noonan's heart leapt. He looked at Katharina and nodded. They carefully descended the staircase and moved to the door. Noonan placed his hand on the ornate handle. There was a girl behind the door! It sounded like Anna! Noonan pressed down on the door handle. The door opened inwards a fraction. Noonan pressed his eye up to crack in the door. A white corridor stretched away. Noonan turned to Katharina, indicating silence. He gently pushed the door opened.

Noonan and Katharina pressed themselves against the sides of the door. Noonan peered round and found himself looking down a long subterranean corridor with doors on either side. The walls, ceiling and floor were all painted brilliant white.

She was here! In one of the rooms! His heart raced. He almost ran into the corridor, pulling at the first door on the right. Katharina remained at the door, covering the corridor. The door swung open. There was a white barred door beyond, and beyond that a white, rectangular, and sterile room, like a hospital room, or a room in a convent. There was an arch window high in the white wall from which artificial light shone, and an iron bed in one corner of the room.   Sitting on her knees on the bed, wearing a simple white dress, was a young woman in her late twenties.   She had straggly, messy, blond hair and her face was gaunt and pale.   He eyes looked up at him, empty and uncomprehending.   She would have been attractive in any other situation but that was being slowly eroded away from her.   Noonan looked her over and could not mistake the red blobs on her wrist from where she had been repeatedly injected with hard drugs.   He took in the pitiful scene, anger rising in his stomach.

"Noonan!"   Katharina's   voice suddenly shrieked behind him.   Noonan wheeled instantly around.   For a moment he took in the black, swarthy features of the man leaning out of the door at the end of the corridor.   He took in the snarling mouth,   the   black   clothes,   the   man's murderous   expression   behind   the   ugly snout of the heavy Colt Government pistol. The twin shots exploded as one with an ear-shattering intensity.   The man's body fell back into the room behind the half open door,   the   pistol   discharging   a   shot. Noonan ducked, the bullet singing past his ear   and   crashing   into   the   white   wall behind him.   For a moment Noonan was frozen to the spot; the action had taken two seconds, but Noonan saw it playing out in his mind in long, fluid, slow motion. He turned to Katharina, who stood framed in the doorway, the smoking pistol in both hands. The spent cartridges rolled across the polished, white, marble floor. The girl in the cell started screaming frantically with ear-splitting intensity. Katharina looked over at Noonan, relief flooding across her face. Noonan closed his eyes for a second, a sick feeling rising in his stomach. He should have been dead. He opened his eyes again and looked at her.

"Thank you," he said, quietly. The girl in the room continued to scream. He ran shakily to the door at the end, his gun raised. He pulled the door open gently and peered round. The body was in a crumpled heap, the right leg twisted awkwardly over the left. It did not stir. Noonan stepped carefully into the room. It was a small room with just a table in the centre, with an ashtray containing four cigarette butts. Noonan placed both feet on either side of the dead mercenary, looking down at him. He bent down and began to search the man, coming up with a brown leather wallet in the man's right hand hip pocket.

Opening it, Noonan found the wallet stuffed full of ten-pound notes. He counted £500 and slipped the wallet into his hip pocket. Both he and Katharina would need operating money and it was worth nothing now to the dead man. Turning the body over, he found a set of keys in the pocket of the leather jacket, which he grasped in his hand. Without giving the mercenary's body another glance, Noonan stepped back into the corridor. Katharina was pressed against the wall a few feet away, looking anxiously up and down the corridor. She turned to him. Noonan raced back to the first door where he had seen the first girl, clasping the keys in his hand. Her screams had subsided, and she now sobbed intermittently. He looked again at the girl through the white bars.

"Is it her?" he vaguely heard Katharina's voice ask him. He just stared into the girl's eyes. "Is it her?" she repeated impatiently. He turned to her then, his expression blank. He just shook his head once.

"No," he simply replied.

Katharina peered into the cell at the girl. "Christ," she muttered under her breath. "What goes on here?" Noonan did not answer but started to try all the keys on the door. Eventually the lock snapped open, and the white barred door swung backwards.

"It's over," Noonan told the girl in the cell. "You can go home." But the girl was neither hearing nor understanding. She simply continued to sob and wail, all the while scratching at her arm.

"Anna!" Noonan yelled down the corridor. He raced to the opposite door and yanked it open. Beyond the bars was another young woman with the same marks on her arms, the tell-tale signs of repeated injections of hard drugs. He unlocked the door once again, but the girl just sat on the end of the bed, vacantly giggling at him.

There were fourteen cells altogether, five of them occupied. There was a man in the third cell who had the distinguished look of a politician. He was huddled naked in one corner of his cell, clutching his knees, and whimpering like a child. The familiar blobs lined the veins on his left arm. The fourth cell contained a young Irishman. His dark cell was being bombarded with strobe lights which pierced Noonan's eyes. The young man was screaming out. Holding a hand up to his face, he raised the gun and fired once. The light cut out in a shower of sparks. The fifth cell contained an African man in white pyjamas. He was lying stretched out across a bed on his stomach. He lifted his head as Noonan opened the door, his white eyes staring unseeingly up at him. He recognised the grey tufts of hair on the chin and the careful, studious eyes from the newspapers. The pungent smell of urine hit Noonan's nostrils. A round, wide stain spread out across the sheets and a puddle had formed on the white floor. The man opened his mouth, but no words came out. He just shook his head once and it fell back onto the pillow.

"Dr Julius Obana," Noonan murmured to himself. "The one they're all looking for." Noonan left all the cell doors unlocked for the patients, but none of them made a move to free themselves. He turned to Katharina, desperation flooding his face.

"She's here!   She must be here!"
He began to feverishly unlock the
remaining nine doors.   But all the empty
cells just stared dumbly back at him.   At
the end, he reeled away, slamming his fists
into the wall.

"NO!" he screamed once.   But then
Katharina was in his face, grabbing his
wrists and pinning them together.

"Noonan, stop it!" she yelled,
leaning heavily into his face.   "She's not
here!"   Noonan looked hard into her eyes,
getting lost in them.   "We must think
about Lomax now!"

He nodded once and she let him go.
He picked up the suitcase and walked back
down the corridor, feeling utterly drained.
Katharina came up alongside him and
gently pressed her body against his.   They
climbed the stairs and back up to the
ground floor.   The portraits on either side
of the corridor stared imperiously down at
them, as if aware of everything that had
been going on.

They opened every door along the
corridor.   One revealed an opulent library
with a desk at the end, with a golden desk
lamp switched on.   Books stretched up to

the ceiling against both walls. A white and golden telephone stood beside the lamp in what appeared to be Lomax's personal study. They walked in briskly, Katharina shutting the door behind her. Noonan whipped up the telephone receiver and hurriedly dialled the number that Spender had drummed into his memory. He pressed the receiver into his ear. The line purred harshly twice, followed by a click, and then Spender's voice, urgent, angry, tired, impatient, rasped sharply in his ear.

"Noonan? What's going on? You're a wanted man!"

"Spender."

There was a pause.

"We had an agreement, Noonan. Why did you renege?"

"I haven't reneged. We still have an agreement."

"You were to go through with the robbery and bring Lomax out with you as ordered. Why didn't you?"

"Because Lomax got away from me. I had nothing to trade. I'm in a stronger position to deal now."

"Where's the box?"

"I've got it. And you can have Lomax with it. He's on his way here now. In return I want you to bring Anna. Also, I want free passage for Miss Vogel to enter another country. And one more thing: you come alone; no police, no helicopters, or the deal's off. You won't see the box again. Understand?"

"Where are you?"

"You'll find out soon enough. Have you got Anna?"

"Yes, she's with me now."

"Then put her on."

But there was just silence at the end of the phone. Finally, Spender's lazy drawl came back to him. "No, Noonan. First you tell me where you are."

"You first, Spender. Where are you and Anna?"

"Don't mess me around, Noonan, you tell me..."

"I'm going to hang up, Spender."

"Alright! We're at Oldershaw Manor Park. It's in Gloucestershire." Noonan felt his body go numb. He said nothing. He heard a familiar click on the other end of the line; the call was being traced. "Noonan?" Spender's voice rasped impatiently.

Noonan hurriedly slammed the receiver down and looked at Katharina, worry flashing across his face.

"Spender's set us up," he told her quietly. "We need to get out of here!"

24

"How do you know he's setting up?" Katharina pressed. "I thought you had a deal."

"He says he's here and that the girl's with him." They ran back down the corridor and came to a familiar door standing open. Katharina quickly recognised the staircase and the passageway beyond it that had been their access into the house. Noonan and Katharina took the steps four or five at time and crashed to the bottom. They made their way along the passageway to the door at the end. They stopped and Noonan carefully opened the door, scanning the lawn stretching away in darkness towards the woods. There was no sign of anyone. Noonan nodded to Katharina, and they started running hard across the lawn.   Suddenly, the lawns were lit up as brightly as a football stadium at night. Noonan looked around, momentarily dazzled.

"Noonan!" he heard Katharina shout and felt her pushing him out of the way with her arms, knocking him to the ground.   He looked up helplessly as Katharina raised her gun at a dark silhouette standing a distance away. The two shots rang out harshly across the lawn, and he watched in horror as her body pirouetted in the air and fell backwards. Her body crashed to the grass, she cried out once, rolling to her side, and then lay still.   Noonan lay frozen for a second, staring into her dying eyes.   He saw surprise there, then fear; a moment later, he saw calm acceptance, then it was as though two twin lights had been switched off in both eyes.   Her head fell slightly forward, and she lay still. But then he was suddenly rolling away as a bullet thudded near to his head.   There was a balustrade several feet away. Noonan glanced up and saw the lone silhouette of Lomax standing on the lawn about fifty metres away, framed against the harsh light, his gun raised.   He picked himself up, holding up the suitcase as a shield with his left hand and firing wildly with his right. He made it to the balustrade and dived over it, landing painfully on the other side, and rolling behind a pillar for cover. He peeped carefully out and looked around. Flood lights positioned all along the roof and the balconies of the house were throwing blinding light down onto the lawn. They were also positioned around the perimeter of the gardens. Another bullet suddenly smashed into the pillar a few inches from his head and Noonan ducked his head back.

"Lomax!" Noonan shouted, a terrible anger throbbing up within him. "You're finished! You hear me?" He listened but heard nothing.

"I just want the box, Noonan!" Lomax's voice came back, ripping across the lawn. "Throw it out now, and it all ends!"

Noonan started crawling along the balustrade to the next pillar, which was thicker and provided better cover. Once he was there, he looked out across the lawn. It was now empty apart from Katharina's lonely body stretched out on its side, the right arm reaching out for something it was never going to grasp. She looked as if she had just fallen asleep on the lawn. Noonan forced her out of his thoughts for now. But what of Lomax? He would be working his way towards him through the trees. Noonan looked wildly around. He needed to make for the cover of the woods, which were about two hundred metres away on the edge of the lawn. An arbour punctuated with stone statues lay between himself and safety, like a final obstacle course. Noonan poised himself, ready to make the dash to the nearest statue. He sprinted over to it, always keeping his head down. He dived behind it as a bullet smashed into the head, causing it to come toppling down on to Noonan's leg. Noonan rolled again and began crawling desperately to a neatly trimmed hedge a few feet away, six feet high, pushing the suitcase out in front of him. He rolled behind it and stood up, crouching.

The hedges formed various paths going off to the left, the right and straight ahead. Noonan started crawling along the edges, looking around all the time. He made it to the junction and looked down the path that stretched towards the woods. The floodlights threw harsh light on every corner and there were no shadows to provide adequate cover.   A stone fountain stood in the middle of the path between the hedges.   Noonan kept his eyes focused on it as he crept forward.   And then the fountain moved!   Noonan raised the gun and fired three times as Lomax stepped out from behind it, returning covering fire. Several chunks of stone exploded outwards.   Noonan ran for the hedge, holding the suitcase out in front of him, and threw himself over it, Lomax's bullets whipping at his feet.   Leaves and branches smashed into his face, one twig catching the edge of his right eye, momentarily blinding him.   He furiously rubbed it and crawled away.   When his vision had returned, he found himself in some sort of shrubbery.   There was a gap in the hedge several feet away.   If he could get behind Lomax...

He crawled to the gap, pushing the suitcase in front of him, raised himself into a crouch and peered around. Yes! Lomax was standing with his back to him, his head moving from left to right, questing. Noonan raised the gun, his finger tightening on the trigger. Then suddenly the world went black. Noonan dropped to his stomach. He lay frozen there for a moment, wondering what had happened. Then the lights came back on again, but, predicably, Lomax was nowhere in sight.

"Nice tactics there, Noonan," Lomax's voice called out to him from a distance away, but Noonan could not tell from where exactly. "But not good enough. You're not going to make it out of here!" Noonan almost shouted back but that would have given away his position. He looked down the path that rolled downwards towards the woods. This path was too obvious. Lomax would be watching it. Noonan backed back into the shrubbery and crawled along the grass. It was tempting to crawl through the shrubbery but that would have made too much noise and alerted Lomax to his position. He made it to a path walled by rhododendron bushes. He got to his feet and padded silently forward, keeping to the edge. At the end, he could see the woods one hundred meters away. Noonan could make it in ten seconds. But that was a long time where Lomax was involved. He peeped around the rhododendron leaves.   A shot exploded out of the darkness, the bullet ripping through the leaves above his head.

"It's over, Noonan!" Lomax's voice called out. "Give up now!" Noonan turned back down the rhododendron path, taking a path going off to the left.   He crawled underneath the leaves at the edge of the path, dragging the suitcase in with him. He felt the cool leaves on his warm face and stared up into the black void, his ears listening hard.   He would have to draw Lomax out by lying here for as long as was necessary.

He had no idea how long he had been lying there before he heard it: the ominous, rumbling sound of a helicopter filling the air, hovering above the house. He pushed himself out so that his head was clear of the bush and looked upwards.   A big white eye was casting around in the deep black sky, getting larger all the time. The tremor was quickly compounded by the distant wailing of police sirens sounding from the front of the house.   The helicopter was rapidly lowering itself to the lawn, the sound building to a terrible crescendo in Noonan's ears.   This had to be Spender. This was his chance!   With

Lomax being forced to run now, he might be able to make it to the woods. He felt the helicopter landing on the main lawn. Noonan pushed himself out of his hiding place and started running as hard as he could towards the cover of the shadows and the woods beyond. He became aware of blurry, moving silhouettes emerging from the darkness on all sides around him. He heard a whistle blow somewhere to the left.

He turned quickly and saw several figures in military green pouring out of the woods on either side of him, closing in. A single report exploded out of the night, but the shot went wide. Noonan bared his teeth and grimaced, peering out through the slits in his eyes. He counted off the distance in his mind, bobbing and weaving towards the woods.

Fifty metres...

Thirty...

Another shot rang out. Noonan ducked and weaved. That time he heard the bullet ring close to his ear. *Go, damn you, go, go!*

Fifteen meters...

Five...

And then the blackness of the woodland grabbed him and pulled him. He heard a body crashing through the undergrowth about ten yards away to his left, moving in a parallel line with him. He glanced quickly and could just make out the figure of Lomax, also running for his life. But he was moving steadily away from him, and his body was quickly swallowed up by the blackness around him. Then he could only hear his own body running. Behind him he heard bodies crashing through the undergrowth in pursuit and raised voices. The darkness behind him began to be lit up with torches.

Still, he ran, no longer aware of a terrible pain that was ripping through his body. All he knew was that he would not stop running until his body finally could take no more. His speed dropped as exhaustion kicked in, but still he refused to stop.

He ran until the voices behind him could no longer keep up with him; he ran out of the woods, across ploughed fields, he ran until he could no longer take in where he was or how far he had come; he ran and ran until, finally, his legs caved in, his lungs collapsed, and he crawled several feet towards the comforting shelter of a bush. He dragged his weary, defeated body underneath the deciduous shrub, making sure that his body and feet were not visible. The short, flattened leaves fanned delicately against his burning, damp face. His breath came out in desperate, angry stabs. He clutched the suitcase hard to his chest, hanging on to it for dear life. It was the only thing that was keeping him alive. He closed his eyes then, images of Anna and Katharina dancing across his subconscious, ghosts in the wild, wintry wilderness, keeping him alive, reminding him of who he was and what he had to do. These feverish thoughts catapulted across his exhausted mind until, quite suddenly, he lost consciousness and dropped gratefully into black, empty space.

25

One week later, Noonan boarded the Lufthansa aircraft from Dublin Airport to Seattle, USA at half past eleven in the morning. He found his seat next to the window and sat down. His head ached. It had been a rough two weeks and he had not slept properly for seventy-two hours.

He had tipped his seat back and closed his eyes, hoping to catch up on the sleep that he had lost out on. The background ambiance of the plane continually bled into his ears: children shrieking, mothers trying to calm their over-excited offspring and the occasional, calm announcement from the captain, a voice of quiet reason in dulcet Irish tones amid an ocean of noisy chaos. Noonan managed to sleep for some of the time but was continually awoken by the anarchy going on around him.   He reflected morosely on the previous week.

Having escaped from Spender and Lomax, he had walked to the nearest town, whence he managed to get a lift with a truck driver to the nearest railway station. From there, he had travelled by train to Liverpool, a journey which had taken the best part of three hours.   With a flat cap pulled down over his eyes, he had tilted his head back and played the part of a sleeping man all the way there.   He had attracted no-one's attention.   Liverpool had been cold and grey, its sombre streets bombarded by furious rain.   Noonan had sheltered in an underpass throughout the night, sharing it with an old tramp with a bottle in a brown paper bag, who paid him no mind.   He waited for the dark hours to tick slowly by, listening to the ferocious rain hammering against the dark pavements outside.   All the time, sprawled on the ground with his back to the cold stone wall, he kept the suitcase clamped against his legs, his right hand gripping the handle.   He could not afford a moment's sleep, could not afford to release his grip on the suitcase.

The following day he had travelled by bus to Liverpool docks and booked a seat on the ferry to Dublin. He did not much feel like sitting down though. Instead, he stayed on deck, his flat cap pulled down, leaning over the barrier, and watching the Liverpool docks gradually diminishing into foggy greyness. The suitcase containing the box was always between his feet. He leaned over the barrier, watching the slosh and froth of the grey, murky waters as the ferry ploughed through them. All the while the chilly, icy winds blew around his ears with a ferocious howl. He stared straight into them and felt their thundering blast on his face, which exhilarated him and cleared his mind. No-one else joined him on the deck, which pleased him. Icy drops of rain began to spit into his eyes. He thought of Katharina then and found himself unexpectedly determined to avenge her death. He owed it to her; she had saved his life twice. She was the second woman to have done so in the space of a few months. She had killed women and children for a cause that meant nothing to him yet in her final living moments had sacrificed her own life to save his. He could spend the rest of his life trying to understand why but would never be able to. He reached into his overalls then and removed one of the passports. He opened it and looked down into the dark-eyed, attractive face of Jean, masquerading as Susan Farmer, the woman Katharina Vogel had been destined never to become. With her dark, thick hair and large, seductive eyes, she could have passed for Katharina's sister. They might have got away with the deception. However, it had been Susan Farmer's fate never to leave the mainland. With a twinge of sadness, Noonan tossed the passport over the side and watched it drop onto the grey, heaving, murky water. He watched it rise on the waves for a moment and then it was gone.

It was a long, cold, tedious journey, eight hours in full, and they did not arrive in Dublin until late in the evening. Earlier on, as the darkness had drawn in, he had had to go indoors and buy a sandwich from the bar, his stomach now aching with hunger.

He began to relax when he eventually disembarked at Dublin, cold and shivering. He hung around the docks, which would have to serve as his dormitory for the night. Despite having crossed the

Irish Sea, he could not risk a hotel; Spender's reach would be considerable. Once again, he stayed awake throughout the dark, lonely hours, this time completely alone, not even a fellow tramp for company. Like the previous night, the suitcase stayed firmly clamped between his legs. He was surprised to find that he was sorely missing Katharina and wishing she was with him now. On such a baleful night, he yearned for her company and the reassuring warmth of her body. In the morning, he breakfasted in a nearby transport café and, requiring an outfit to suit the kind of character he wanted to be when he reached his destination, bought a white suit from a nearby department store. He had spent much of the night studying Brewster's passport, and thinking himself into the role of John Davidson, the man whose identity Brewster was to have assumed. They were of a similar age, but Noonan would need to alter his appearance sufficiently to pass for Brewster/Davidson. To that purpose, he would require the services of a hairdresser. He found one down a side street and asked the young, blond, attractive Irish girl to arrange his hair in a bouffant style that would be a fair approximation of Brewster's. She did a superb job, and as Noonan looked into the mirror, he saw a fair impression of Brewster/Davidson staring back at him. He did not look much like Brewster, but the height and haircut might be enough to carry off the deception. The rest he would have to put down to luck, fate, and the thoroughness of the passport official he would eventually be dealing with. If he got rumbled, it would all be finished for him. He would just have to brave it out. John Davidson would have to see it through the bitter end.

From there, he took a taxi to Dublin Airport and booked his flight. He found the row of lockers and placed the suitcase squarely in one of them, in the middle of the second row down. He glanced down at his key, numbered '346'. He slammed the door, locking it. He pulled at it hard several times, but the locker, and the suitcase within it, were firmly secure. He then found a seat near the lockers and began the long four hour wait until his flight, keeping the key scrunched up into his fist. He pulled his cap down over his eyes and kept his eyes on the lockers. He had kept sleep at bay for nearly three days but now it was coming round to collect with a vengeance. His eyelids felt as heavy as coins and his head kept falling forward, his body willing him to sleep. But every time he shook himself awake and desperately refocused his gaze onto the lockers. Travellers roamed around his locker or just walked past it, paying it no mind. A small, wiry young Irishman with long, lank hair, a black leather jacket and a drooping moustache then appeared in his peripheral vision. He was carrying a briefcase and was looking furtively around. Noonan's body straightened and his mind cleared. Everything about the young man spelled trouble. He moved slowly up to Noonan's locker and glanced around again. Noonan tensed, ready to pounce on the rodent-like young man. But he just opened the locker to the left of Noonan's, slipped the briefcase inside, twisted the key, walked smartly away with it, and was gone. At one point, Noonan realised he had dropped into sleep for only a matter of seconds, and was only awoken, mercifully, by the screams of a young boy sitting with his long-suffering mother several chairs away from him. He kept his eyes on the locker, ticking the minutes off in his mind.

When it was finally time to move to the departure lounge, he took his place in the queue. He counted the passengers down until he found himself being studied by the indifferent eyes of the passport official, the final hurdle along this seemingly endless and treacherous journey. And so it was that John Davidson stared confidently back into the man's dour, middle-aged, tired, disinterested face. His eyes must have been bloodshot through lack of sleep and his chin itched with the start of a beard. But John Davidson had nothing to hide. The man glanced down at the passport photograph and then looked back at Noonan for several seconds. The man would never have known it, but Noonan's heart was thumping inside him with such ferocity that Noonan might have sworn that the other passengers queuing around him could hear it. After what felt like half a minute the man fixed an impersonal smile on his face, murmured "Thank you, Mr Davidson," and handed the passport back. Noonan was thrown for less than a second at being called by a different name, instantly recovered it, smiled back, took the passport, and walked confidently in line with the other passengers towards the departure lounge, thanking his good fortune. He dropped the locker key into his shoe.

The plane landed in Seattle five hours later, where they were allowed to stretch their legs and grab a drink at a bar. Noonan was in no mood to drink however, so bought himself a steak instead from a canteen. It was perfunctorily cooked, but it filled him up. All he could see of Seattle through the tall airport window was a grey, murky sky with drizzle floating out of it. That was as much of Seattle as he wanted to see.

They boarded the plane for the second part of their journey, which took them all the way to Maui, another fizzy five-hour cocktail of shrieks, laughter, calm announcements from the drawling pilot, and the return of the eternal headache. He had asked for an aspirin from the blond, doll-like stewardess, "Gloria" according to her name badge. She had smiled and told him it was coming right up. An hour later, she finally got back to him with it. Noonan decided that he hated flying and would never to do it again if he could help it.

Finally, the ordeal came to an end, and he was stepping out onto the runway at Maui, dressed in his white suit and wearing a pair of mirrored sunglasses that he had bought in Seattle. The ferocious heat of Maui blasted him the moment he stepped off the plane. Things were no cooler in Maui airport, and he edged his way closer to Arrivals, finally getting the stamp on his passport and making his way through the sliding door. He hired a car, a 1963 Chevrolet Corvair, with the roof down, and found his way to a low-class hotel. It suited his purpose, as he had come to this place in the guise of a lowlife with criminal connections. If he was going to succeed at what he was setting out to do, it was the company of criminals he would need to seek out. Noonan took out the wallet that he had stolen from Oldershaw Manor Park, counted the money that he had left over, and dropped it on the bed. He sat down next to it and looked up at the ceiling fan. The problem was how to hide the locker key, but he thought he had the answer. He stepped out into the corridor outside, looking carefully up and down. All was quiet. He took one of the wooden chairs lined along the corridor and placed it underneath one of the ceiling lights. He stood on the chair, lowered the plastic cover, carefully hid the key, replaced the cover, stepped down, replaced the chair, and headed back to his room. The ceiling fan was still rotating. He suddenly felt very alone. He lay back on the bed and instantly fell into a long, restful sleep from which he felt he might never wake up.

The following morning Noonan took his money back to the airport, exchanging the currency for dollars, which now amounted to $400. In the evening he explored the night life and the dingy bars, seeking out the local underworld. He could usually spot them straight away.

The bar was by the water with a young topless dancer on a bamboo stage. Hawaiian guitars rang out from an all-smiling band playing in the corner. He spotted the quartet around the card table over on the sand and knew instantly they were the ones he was looking for. He sauntered over and flashed his money. Their fierce eyes glittered with suspicion. He explained what he was in the market for. The leader of the gang introduced himself as Fidel. They kept him waiting for an hour while they finished their game, then led him to an abandoned shed, where they started to work him over. He put two of them on the ground within seconds, after which they were more willing to talk business. He parted with $150, and they parted with a Remington 700 bolt action rifle and a Smith & Wesson Model 10 revolver. He locked the firearms in the boot of the Chevrolet and drove back to the hotel.

The following afternoon, he went to the City Hall to look for all the information he could find on Lomax's hideaway. He was shown an aerial map of the area. Lomax's luxury home, Kahiau, was on a peninsula at the rugged, wild, far end of the island. A small fishing community lived close to the peninsula under a magnificent set of waterfalls. As evening was starting to set in, he checked out of the hotel and drove to the far end of the island. On the way he stopped at a gas station, bought six fuel canisters, and filled them up with gasoline. He parked the car off the road in a grove of trees and walked the final quarter mile.

The villagers, most of them male and in their twenties and early thirties,

342

greeted him warmly and offered him their local beer. He accepted their hospitality and then showed them his money, offering $100 to anyone with a boat who might be willing to take him around the peninsula. They eyed him suspiciously then and most started shaking their heads. Finally, the youngest looking, probably no more than fifteen years old, snatched his money, and told him he could take him now. Noonan readily agreed, but only on condition that they made their journey at night. And so, as the path of the moon cut across the Pacific, they set off across the calm, aquamarine waters.

Noonan looked up at the peninsula and saw the black bulk of the house. They would barely be visible in the dark, but there was a point around the far side of the peninsula when they would have been out of sight of the house completely. They gently floated past it before it disappeared, the two of them in the boat. When the boat came round the other side and was heading back to the village, there was just the boy in it.

<u>26</u>

The waves lapped at Leilani's feet. Her eyes were closed, and her head lay on her arms. Lomax had returned two days earlier and been in a particularly ugly mood since. The job he had returned to England to do, the final job, had clearly not gone the way he had planned. Inevitably he had taken his fury out on her in his usual, vicious way. The month that he had been away had been a blessed respite, but it had ended all too soon. And the boy, Keonaoma, was always far worse when his master was around.

The sun breathed its heavenly warmth onto Leilani's back. But even the sun had become just another unrelenting, malevolent companion during this unending nightmare. She no longer found comfort in it, nor did the sweet sensation of

344

the water on her skin send any pleasure through her body. It was around five o'clock in the afternoon. She could tell simply from the position of the sun and whereabouts it hung in the sky. That would mean the boy would be along soon. This was the time he usually appeared.

Leilani looked up. The two Frenchmen were seated at the far end of the beach, far enough away for them not to intrude on her privacy, but near enough that they could still an keep an eye on her. They had their shoulder holsters strapped across their chests and were throwing cards down on a small table in between them. The Maui parrotbills fluttered in her ears from the trees surrounding the beach. It was then she heard his ghastly, crowing, sing-song voice floating down to her from the top of the beach.

"Angel..."

She buried her heard in her arms and refused to move. She then heard the crack of his new toy, a bullwhip, which he had started tormenting her with, using it to make her run faster up to the house, giggling like a child as he did so.

"Angel..." he crowed a second time. She dug the palms of her hands into the sand. It was time to get up. She must not give him that satisfaction. She got to her feet and walked briskly towards him, refusing to look in the eye. She made out as if she was heading back up to the house anyway. The closer she got to him, the more he started to crack his whip, as if in anticipation of the events of the evening. She came within ten feet of him. The whip came down. *Crack!* Five feet. Another *crack*, harder this time.

C-RACK!

The sound of the rifle firing exploded across the beach. The Maui parrotbills exploded from the palm trees and flapped away in terror. Leilani's heart seemed to leap out of her at the sudden, terrifyingly loud sound. She looked up in shock and screamed. The bullet had torn through Keonaoma's right cheek bone and had ripped away a huge chunk of the left side of his face. The scream throbbed up from the depths of her soul, an ear-shattering, blood-curdling scream. Her fist came up to her mouth and the terror then came out in sobs. Keonaoma's lifeless body flopped to the sand, instantly dead.

346

Leilani threw herself down, her body shivering with horror despite the heat.

Across the beach, the two French bodyguards dropped their cards at the sound of the shot. They glanced across and saw the boy's body falling. Their hands clumsily fumbled for the heavy calibre revolvers at their arms and ripped them out. They glanced all around but could see no sign of the intruder. They raised the guns and fired several times into the surrounding trees, then turned and started running for cover.

C-RACK!

The second bullet smacked through the back of the first man's head, slapping his body violently to the sand. The second man nearly made it to the trees before another bullet caught him dead centre between the shoulder blades. His body pitched forward, the head and arms rising to the sky, as if in prayer to the Almighty. Then it came crashing face down into the sand.

The shooting stopped. Leilani lifted her body but remained on her knees. She was unable to stop shaking. She crossed her arms across her torso, the sobs of terror choking from her. Nothing moved on the beach for thirty seconds. Then she was aware of a pair of white suit trousers and brown leather shoes moving delicately towards her. They stopped a few feet in front of her. What did this mean? Was she about to be killed too? She plucked up the courage to look at the intruder's face. She had expected to see a face like Lomax or the two Frenchmen.   His face was different though.   While the skin was similarly   taut   and   craggy,   it   was unexpectedly pale, the skin of someone who had come here from a different part of the world; the eyes were unusually soft and compassionate.   He dropped down to his knees, resting the rifle across them, and looked at her, the barrel pointing vaguely in her direction.

"It's alright. I won't hurt you if you help me." The voice was soft, but with an edge to it.   She nodded once.   "Where's Lomax?"   She pointed a quivering figure up to the house. "Take me to him."

She nodded, and she felt her heart begin to throb with relief. She had prayed for the arrival of this man for months and unbelievably he was suddenly now here. She got slowly, nervously, to her feet and led him towards the trees, to a place where she had frequently gone on many previous occasions to hide. Noonan followed her warily, the canisters in his hands and the rifle pointing at her back. Their bodies vanished into the trees.

Lomax, also dressed in a white suit, had heard the shots from the upper lawn. Instantly he had shot up from his iron table, where he had been enjoying a black coffee, and had raced back into the house. He locked the back door, then ran through the house, locking all the doors and windows, before racing up the ornate staircase to the first floor. He dived into the vast, white bedroom, got down on his knees and pulled back a section of the carpet. He lifted a section of the wooden floor and pulled out a long leather case that had been hidden there. He opened this and pulled out an M16A1 automatic rifle, slamming a 30-round magazine into it. He reached back into the floor and pulled out four spare magazines. He stood up, shoving the magazines into his jacket pocket. He moved to the window and peered carefully out. There was nothing moving outside.

Lomax left the bedroom and crept quietly through the upstairs, stopping in the various rooms to peer out of the windows, his finger always taut on the trigger of the M16A1. The silence rained down on him. He waited for ten minutes for the inevitable crash of glass and the accompanying home invasion. Fifteen minutes. But they never came. Who were his assailants? Were they playing a waiting game? Or was it just one man? Then he realised. He knew. And the ghost of a smile played across his face.

He then heard it, the distant smash and tinkle of glass. Then he heard nothing. He quietly opened the door of the spare bedroom and looked down the long landing, raising the M16A1 and looking down its barrel. But he heard nothing more and saw no-one.

He sniffed cautiously. Had the cook left something in the oven? He could smell burning. Then the terrible realisation hit him. He could see the smoke now. It was billowing up to him from the ground floor, gusts of it, like a thick fog. Lomax started to cough, and his eyes quickly started stinging. He ran further back along the landing, but the

350

smoke was even thicker coming from that direction. A minute later he was struggling to see ahead of him. The smoke was getting deep into his lungs now and he was coughing and spluttering painfully. He had to get out of here! He edged to the top of the staircase and looked down. The entire ground floor was ablaze, fire spreading rapidly across the entire width of the house, burning with a ferocious, infernal orange light. If he tried to get through that he would be burned to a crisp! And in less than two minutes it would have reached the first floor!

Lomax raced back to the master bedroom, holding his breath, and screwing his eyes tight as he did so. He kicked the door open and raced through the room. He lifted the MI6A1 and smashed the glass out of the French windows, collapsing onto the balcony and sucking in a huge lungful of fresh air. He looked over the balcony, but the lawn was now covered with thick smog. It was becoming impossible to see anything. He could see that the exterior of the house was now blackened and enveloped in flames. He lifted his legs over the side and jumped to the ground, landing, and rolling over. He sprung to his feet.   The smoke was swirling all around him, getting into his eyes, getting into his lungs.   He took cover behind the steps leading down into the garden.

The shot came from behind him, the bullet kicking him in the back and ripping a huge hole through his chest.   Lomax's body lurched forward, landing messily at the bottom of the steps.   He looked down to see a wide hole in his stomach, and blood rapidly spreading across his shirt.   He screwed his face up, feeling the blood rising in his throat.   He turned and began walking back to the house, firing all around him as he did so.   He saw a figure advancing towards him with a rifle raised. He turned the M16A1 towards the figure, hitting him with everything he had.   He saw the figure jerk and twist.   But then there came the deep boom of the rifle again and Lomax felt another bullet slam into his chest.   He fell backwards then, the muscles in his hand tightening around the trigger, the M16A1 continuing to scatter bullets across the lawn and towards the ocean.   Then the rifle went silent, and Lomax lay there, the smoke driving into his eyes.   He blinked several times and tried to crawl, but he could make it no further than a few feet. Then out of the smoke a pair of feet stepped in front of him. Lomax's body turned over onto its back. He could see Noonan standing over him with a Smith & Wesson Model 10 revolver aiming down on him. One of his bullets had ripped into his left shoulder. Lomax suddenly lunged up, the flash of a blade suddenly appearing in his hand. With the other hand, he managed push the revolver away. Lomax plunged the knife deep into Noonan's chest. Noonan's body dropped to the ground on top of Lomax's, a cry exploding from his lungs. Despite the pain ripping through his body, he was barely feeling anything. He clamped his hands around Lomax's throat and squeezed. Lomax managed to get his hands around Noonan's throat too, also squeezing. But Noonan was on top, forcing his face down onto Lomax's, grimacing furiously, his eyes blazing. A terrible roar exploded from his guts as he squeezed. At the same time, he felt the air being cut off in his own lungs and his head beginning to swim. But then he saw Lomax's eyes start to dull over and the pressure on his throat start to subside.

Lomax felt no fear. No remorse. Just the same hatred he had always felt at the rest of the world. He lifted his head and tried to spit at Noonan, but he ended up just choking on his own saliva mixed in with his own blood.

Noonan's voice was even, deadly. "Where's Anna?"

Lomax looked up at him, smiling one final, withering smile of contempt.

"Where's Anna!?"

He was looking down into Lomax's face, watching the life being throttled out of it. And then the head fell back, the eyes finally empty. Noonan fell backwards, away from the body. He looked back at it fearfully, but there was no longer any life left in it, just the withering, scornful smile on his face that was to be his final departing message to the world.

Leilani came out of her hiding place and found the two bloodied men, both in white suits, lying beside each other. She had had to run around for several minutes in the thick smoke, coughing and choking, trying to locate them. She knelt by the bodies. Lomax was dead. She stared with defiance into the lifeless eyes of the man who had made her life an unbearable misery over the last two years. Even in death, the eyes bore nothing but disdain at the world they stared unseeingly up at. She then turned her attention to the other man, the man who had come from nowhere to rescue her from all this. He was still alive but in obvious pain. His lips were moving. He was trying to say something to her. She leaned in closer, trying to hear his words.

"Help me," he whispered. She was already on her feet, moving to save both their lives. The fire was spreading across the lawn and would soon devour them. Like most island girls, she was a creature of nature, and had a surprising bodily strength. She was able to pull him to his feet, drape his right arm around her shoulders and pull her away from the infernal smoke. His body was heavy, but she was determined to get him away from this place, even if it was the last thing she ever did.

She took him down a narrow path between the two mountains that led away from the house. She looked back at it one final time, now a blackened, scarred obscenity, burned to a crisp. The flames were now reaching to the sky, lighting the approaching night like a giant, primeval candle. Thick gusts of black smoke belched upwards towards the darkening sky.

She would get him to safety though.

And she would keep him alive.

It was the least she could do for him.

Noonan tried to stay conscious, but he found himself slipping into the familiar black comfort of the void again. He was dimly aware of his body being dragged along on its feet down a hill and the pungent smell of black smoke perforating his nostrils. Back on the mainland he had the distant impression of sirens sounding out and the red and blue flash of lights. He tried in his state to understand the meaning of the lights but before he could make anything of them, his head went back, and he fell again into the unending well of blackness.

<u>27</u>

He was swimming in white milkiness. What had happened to him? His eyes were trying to open, but the light was blinding him, and he had to keep closing them. He saw, or thought he saw, two white angels hovering over him. After what might have been several years later, his eyes had opened again, and he was now able to see the clearly. But they no longer looked like angels. Instead, they began to resemble two severe-looking, unsmiling police officials, looking down on him, peering into his face with mild curiosity.

"I think he's coming round," the nearest one said, his voice echoing. But for Noonan it felt like it was a voice coming to him from another world. He closed his eyes again and fell back into a deep sleep. He was aware that his stomach ached terribly, the pain surging through his body with a mechanical throb. He wanted to stay in the darkness for as long as possible, maybe forever. Anywhere where he would not have to see the two evil angels again. But the darkness had no place for him and quickly ejected him out into the brightness of the police ward at the hospital. The two unsmiling officers were still there. How long had they been there? Hours? Days? Months? This time however they were wearing grim smiles.

"We've got a lot of questions for you, buddy," drawled the one nearest to him, who looked as if he was the senior officer. "What's your name?" He had a grey crew cut, a square face, a taut, solid body, and hard, brown eyes. Noonan held him in his gaze and looked straight through him. He had nothing to say. He was not even in his own country. They had no information on him, and he was carrying no papers. Brewster's passport was in the drawer back at the hotel.

"I said, what's your name, buddy?" The officer asked again. Noonan did not shift his empty gaze.

"You want to play the tough guy, huh?" the second man picked it up. He was a younger man with ginger, wavy hair, and long ginger sideburns. There was no reply. "That's ok, pal. We can handle that too."

This routine continued for the next couple of days. Then at the end of the third day, they finally gave up, and made a move to leave. At the door they turned.

"We've got a nice prison cell waiting for you, buddy," drawled the older officer. "Unless you decide to talk to us. Could make things a lot easier for you."

Noonan had said nothing for two days. He was not about to start now. If he said anything to these men, they could use it against him later. The older officer, with a mischievous twinkle in his eye, shook his head at Noonan and walked away with a casual, "Oh boy, I wouldn't want to be in your shoes, buddy. You're about to go down for the full stretch..." He turned and walked away.

The ginger-haired man, who had a kinder face, remained in the doorway, a slight smile on his face. "Funny thing is you did us all a favour. We've been looking

359

for ways to get rid of that guy legally ever since he showed up." He took a couple of steps forward, his eyes blazing with curiosity. "What are you? British Intelligence? MI6?" Noonan closed his eyes for a second and looked up at the ceiling. The ginger-haired man nodded once more. "Yep – I figured it."

He turned and left the room. When he was well enough to leave the hospital, his chest still burning with excruciating pain from the knife wound, his two friendly companions were waiting to escort him to Police Headquarters and the usual round of questions. He eventually learned their names. The grey haired, older man with the crew cut was Randall H. Batteran and his younger, ginger haired associate was James Auger. They were both CIA and had flown over from the mainland specially to interview him. It had turned out that the American government had been taking an interest in Lomax and had been informed of his death by the local island police, who had detained Noonan as soon as they had recovered his unconscious body from the peninsula. The girl Leilani had been allowed to go back to her people. They had then waited with varying degrees of impatience for Noonan to recover from his knife wound so that they could begin the interviewing process. Noonan learned that he had been under an anaesthetic and operated on for a whole week. At the end of the afternoon's round of questions, after which they had learned nothing new from Noonan, they took him down to a dark, dank cell in the bowels of the Police Headquarters that was to become his new home, for what he assumed would be the immediate future. A beard was starting to grow on his face. The loneliness, the hunger and the desolation set in; but Noonan had had to deal with far worse.

He estimated that he had been there for two whole weeks when the door to his cell slowly opened and Spender's elegant, familiar figure strode smartly in. Batteran and Auger came in behind him, in triangular formation. Noonan was surprised that he was happy to see Spender. Stuck on an unfamiliar island in the middle of the Pacific, at least he felt a connection with this man. This man represented England, Anna, *home*. Then again, he had seen inside the box. What had home really become now?

"Someone to see you, buddy," Randall Batteran said sourly. "He's flown in especially. Says he wants to help you. You'd better listen to what he has to say."

"Thank you," Spender growled haughtily. Batteran glowered angrily for a moment; he could recognise when he was being dismissed and he did not like it one bit.

"I'll be outside," Batteran growled without enthusiasm. Then he turned and closed the cell door behind him. Spender turned to make sure that they could speak privately.

Spender opened with, "Well, then..." He stood and looked at Noonan. "It's not looking good for you, I'm afraid, Noonan. I may not be able to help you this time. Committing acts of violence in a foreign territory with which we have friendly relations. And two dead policemen back in England."

"That was Lomax," Noonan replied. He barely recognised his croaky voice as it spoke; it was the first time he had really heard it in nearly a fortnight.

362

"Maybe," Spender replied calmly. "You still have a chance, Noonan. But that rather depends on you." Noonan waited. "Where's the box?"

"When do I get out of here?" Noonan countered.

"You're in no position to trade." Spender replied.

"Leave me here and you'll never see that box. Only I know where it is. No murder charges, you wipe it all clean."

There was a pause, then Spender spoke slowly, choosing his words carefully. "No promises."

"What do you really intend to do with that box if you get it?"

"It's government property," Spender answered. "It always was. So, we simply must have it."

"Once we'd got away from Lomax, you were going to have the lot of us thrown into prison, weren't you? You've been lying to me right from the start." Noonan's words felt like projectiles in the tiny cell.

"You're wrong about one thing, Noonan. I wasn't lying about Anna." He took a step forward. "I said I would find her for you." Spender slipped a hand into the inside pocket of his overcoat and removed a photograph, handing it to Noonan. Noonan examined it and his heart seemed to beat faster. It was a black and white photograph of Anna. She was sitting at a table, looking distractedly away into the middle distance to her right, but in the background, standing out in absolute clarity was a digital clock. The date and time could be seen clearly: 05/03/1973 – 14:03. The background was hazy, and it looked like there were similar tables positioned all around. It could have been a restaurant or a prison waiting room. The photograph had clearly been taken without her knowledge.

"What's the date today?" Noonan asked.

"March 8th", Spender rasped.

"Three days ago," Noonan calculated. "Where is this?"

"I'm sorry, Noonan, but that's all you get for free." Noonan nodded in understanding. He moved the photograph towards the pocket of his prison overalls, but Spender moved smoothly towards him, taking back the photograph, and holding it over him. "And that stays with me." He replaced the photograph inside his overcoat. Noonan sank back, looking into Spender's eyes. Lomax was dead, but in Spender, Lomax lived on. Only Spender was not a vicious killer like Lomax, he was instead a sadistic, mental chess player. In many ways, that made him even more dangerous than Lomax.

"Lomax, Spender..." Noonan growled. "It still goes on, doesn't it? It always will."

"Hand over the box, and you'll get the girl and all the charges against you dropped. That's the deal. Now I'll be over here for another twenty-four hours," Spender continued, "so don't take too long thinking about it. I'll be back tomorrow morning, for the last time." He turned to the door. "Mr Batteran?"

Batteran appeared a moment later. He unlocked the cell door and Spender stepped smartly through it. Batteran locked the door again. Spender looked at Noonan one last time through the grill.

"I'll be seeing you, Noonan".

And with that, he turned and walked away, his footsteps echoing down the long, dark, stone corridor.

Printed in Great Britain
by Amazon

85162912R00210